She wanted to be alone with him...

The bare bones truth was that Elizabeth wanted Ben to make love to her, touch her, tell her how wonderful she was. Yet here she was in a crowded theater, pretending to watch a movie.

"Is everything okay?" he whispered.

She shifted in her seat. "No. I'd rather be in bed with you, making mad, passionate love."

"Now?" he asked, the light in his dark eyes growing even brighter.

"Now."

His mouth brushed hers before he grabbed the popcorn and stood, pulling her out of her seat. "Excuse me," he said quietly to the couple on the aisle.

In five minutes Ben and Elizabeth were in the car, heading down the road. She couldn't believe she'd really been so forward.

"I'm sorry you didn't get to see the end of the movie," she ventured, feeling suddenly timid.

"In six months we'll rent it." Ben took her hand and placed it on his thigh. "Don't get cold feet on me now, darlin'."

"I'm not," she protested. "I meant what I said. I'm just surprised I said it."

His laugh was husky. "I love a woman who says what's on her mind. Especially when it involves mad, passionate love."

Rita Clay Estrada is a vibrant fixture in the world of romance writing. Not only has she written thirty-three romance novels to date, she created and co-founded the Romance Writers of America, the only organization of its kind in the world. Each year, RITA awards, so named in Rita Clay Estrada's honor, are given to the best and brightest authors published in romance.

Early on, Rita established herself as a bestselling Harlequin Temptation author. Her stories always seem to strike the right emotional chord and fans won't be disappointed by *Everything About Him*. Newcomers to Rita Clay Estrada and loyal readers alike will welcome another "keeper" to the shelf.

Look for Rita's next Temptation novel, #733 *One Wild Weekend*, in June 1999.

Books by Rita Clay Estrada

HARLEQUIN TEMPTATION
573—THE STORMCHASER
595—LOVE ME, LOVE MY BED
634—WISHES
687—DREAMS

Don't miss any of our special offers. Write to us at the following address for information on our newest releases.

Harlequin Reader Service
U.S.: 3010 Walden Ave., P.O. Box 1325, Buffalo, NY 14269
Canadian: P.O. Box 609, Fort Erie, Ont. L2A 5X3

Rita Clay Estrada
EVERYTHING ABOUT HIM

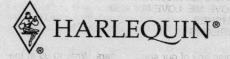

HARLEQUIN®

TORONTO • NEW YORK • LONDON
AMSTERDAM • PARIS • SYDNEY • HAMBURG
STOCKHOLM • ATHENS • TOKYO • MILAN • MADRID
PRAGUE • WARSAW • BUDAPEST • AUCKLAND

For Elizabeth Jean Polce,
better known as Betty Jean Gallagher,
my playmate and friend, youthful idol and aunt.
Beautiful and witty—what a combination!

ISBN 0-373-25813-5

EVERYTHING ABOUT HIM

Copyright © 1999 by Rita Clay Estrada.

This edition published by arrangement with Harlequin Books S.A.

® and TM are trademarks of the publisher. Trademarks indicated with ® are registered in the United States Patent and Trademark Office, the Canadian Trade Marks Office and in other countries.

Printed in U.S.A.

1

UNEXPECTED OR UNWANTED pregnancies were tough on everyone, not just the mother-to-be.

Stroking the young girl's blond hair, Elizabeth Jean Gallagher held her close and let her cry out the hurt, fear and other overwhelming emotions that had tortured her for the past few months. Her name was Barbie Damati. Sixteen, and four months pregnant, she had been hiding her condition until this week, when her father had finally caught on. Then her life changed drastically.

He was the one who'd arranged for Barbie to see Elizabeth to discuss the problems and options. As a psychologist, Elizabeth specialized in dealing with pregnant teens and leading them through the labyrinth of choices available. Barbie's father had meant to come, too, but had called with a business emergency. *Such a dear, involved father*, she thought dryly.

Barbie's voice rasped as she tried to speak, then hiccuped.

"Shh. Just take your time," Elizabeth said softly.

The young girl's thoughts and words were all jumbled up in an emotional whirlwind as, for the first time, she confronted what was happening to her. Elizabeth could only be supportive right now; there was nothing she could say. Not yet. Barbie had to talk before she would listen.

"I don't know what to do anymore! I thought I was eating because I was nervous, and that's why I was gaining weight. But I kept getting heavier and heavier. And then my friend Marsha told me she thought I was pregnant, and I think I knew she was right, but I didn't want to hear it. I yelled at her and screamed all kinds of things. I don't know what I said, but it must have been bad because she won't even talk to me anymore!" Barbie tried to catch her breath, but words still tumbled out as she spilled her feelings. "Even when I apologized, she wouldn't talk to me, and I miss her so much! I didn't mean what I said, whatever it was! And my boyfriend won't talk to me, not since last week, when I told him what the clinic told me. I'm gonna have a baby and no one wants anything to do with me! And when the rest of the kids find out, they'll laugh at me and talk about me behind my back and then I'll be the laughingstock of the school!"

"Hold, it, honey," Elizabeth crooned. "One crisis at a time. Let's talk about what's happening now, not what the future might hold. Not yet, okay?"

"I can't think anymore, Miss Gallagher!" Barbie cried. "I'm so hurt! How could he deny he's the father? He's the only one in my life, ever. And I love him so much!"

"Is he someone from school?" Elizabeth asked.

"Yes—" Barbie gulped back another bout of

tears "—but I can't tell you who he is. My dad will kill him and I can't let that happen."

Elizabeth gave Barbie's shoulder a pat. "Don't you think he ought to share the problems and the joys of this with you?"

"No! Yes!" Barbie's head dropped into her hands. "I don't know. I'm so confused! If I tell on him now, he might not change his mind and be with me later."

"And you really, deep down, think he *will* change his mind?" Elizabeth prodded gently, knowing the chances were practically nil. Most boys, once they had their parents' permission, denied all involvement, usually blaming it on some other boy, saying the girl was having sex with other guys. It was a ploy that everyone recognized, but seldom confronted.

"I don't know, but I can't imagine him doing this to me! He loves me, I know it! And if he doesn't, I'll be ruined!"

"Not ruined, Barbie. But I won't lie to you. The next year won't be easy. No matter what decision you make, your life is going to change."

"All I know is I want to run away. But if I do, my dad will kill me!" She hiccuped again, her arms tightening around Elizabeth's waist. "And if I don't, I think he'll kill me anyway! He's so angry he can't even look at me! And if he ever finds out my boyfriend's name, he'll kill him, too!"

Elizabeth wasn't sure Barbie was ready to begin listening yet, but it was worth a try. "I haven't met your dad, but I'd bet he's not quite that unreasonable."

"Yes, he is! My dad's an architect, and every-

thing is always so precise. So exact. And this isn't any of that." Barbie's head bobbed against Elizabeth's shoulder. "I've seen him angry before, but not like this."

"He's as upset about this as you are because he loves you."

"He'll get meaner, Miss Gallagher. I just don't know what to do!" Barbie wailed, her body shaking with sobs as she clung to the older woman.

Elizabeth continued soothing her young charge. No matter what choices Barbie made, it would be tough going. There was no doubt that because of this mistake in judgment, Barbie was going to grow up faster than the average girl.

Helping young girls in Barbie's situation was what Elizabeth did every day. Many of her patients came as referrals from the school district, the headquarters of which was only two blocks from Barbie's high school. Most of the time there were rewards, sometimes not. And always there was paperwork. Miles and miles of it.

Elizabeth's heart hurt from the anxiety this young girl was going through, and she was wary. Just three months ago, Elizabeth had experienced another scene much like this one, only that time the girl—named Jennifer—had been right. Her father had beat her with a leather belt until she fell, hit her head on the concrete step of the back porch and died. Elizabeth was still too raw to take words like *kill* in stride just because it was thrown about by a teenage girl at a highly emotional moment.

"I'll tell you what, Barbie." Elizabeth leaned down and looked into her young client's face,

grabbing tissues and putting them in her hands as she did so. "It's already after seven, and I bet your parents are worried. I'll call your mom and alert her to the problem, then I'll meet with your parents tomorrow."

Barbie hiccuped yet again. "I didn't tell you earlier, but I don't have a mom. She died when I was eleven." Her face collapsed again in tears. "I wish I did. I wish I had a mom who cared and listened to me. Who made us a family again."

Elizabeth took a deep breath and kept her mind on the task at hand. It wasn't going to help if she was overcome with pity. "I'll call your dad and wait here until he picks you up. I'm sure that once we talk, he'll be more than reasonable."

"He doesn't care! All he wants to do is find the father and beat him up so he can get on with his career!"

"Now, Barbie," Elizabeth began, but the girl's crying started up again. "Bring your father here tomorrow. I'll talk to him."

Barbie raised her blond head and looked up, her wide blue eyes glistening with tears. "You don't understand, Miss Gallagher. He's already angry. According to him the only time you need this kind of help is if you're crazy! He just made this appointment because he didn't know what else to do with me!"

"Oh, really?" Elizabeth felt her spine stiffen. "And what's his idea of help?"

"I don't know, but I'm so scared, Miss Gallagher." Barbie closed her eyes and gave a shudder.

Elizabeth began searching for alternatives.

"Are there *any* women in the house? An aunt? A stepmother? Your grandmother?"

"No. It's just the two of us." Barbie sounded so forlorn it almost broke Elizabeth's heart.

"Give me his number." It was an order. Slowly, the girl complied. Elizabeth grabbed a pencil, jotted down the number and dialed the phone on her desk. She went through a receptionist, then a secretary, who referred her to his private assistant. Obviously the man was busy, but that didn't mean she couldn't interrupt. When his assistant came on the line, Elizabeth asked for Mr. Damati and was told he was in a long meeting and probably wouldn't be free until midnight. Was it an emergency?

What could she say? He already knew his daughter's condition. He already knew the problems his daughter was facing. He had to know the fear she was experiencing. And yet he was in a meeting that would last until midnight, leaving his child alone to fend for herself.

The louse.

"May I have his voice mail?" she asked, barely able to hold back the venom she felt over his callousness.

When it came on, she gave her message. "Mr. Damati, this is Elizabeth Gallagher, the psychologist you were supposed to have an appointment with this afternoon. Your daughter is sitting in my office, very upset, and rightfully so. I've just found out that you're too busy to come to the phone or pick up your daughter this evening, so I'm taking her home with me for the night. You can page me and I'll return your call immediately. Meanwhile, I'll make sure she has dinner and see she gets some rest." She gave her beeper number and hung up with a snap.

Barbie's big blue eyes looked up at her as if she were an angel. "You're taking me home with you?"

"Yes." She reached for her purse. She had just crossed a line—she had to keep distance between herself and "her girls"—but it was too late. They were already on the path, so she might as well continue. "Grab your books and let's go."

For the first time since their meeting began, Barbie smiled. "Yes, ma'am." But under her breath she said what Elizabeth already felt. "I think my dad just met his match."

On the way home, Elizabeth stopped at a fast-food place and treated both of them to hamburgers. There was nothing in the fridge, and sometime this week she'd be forced to do her monthly grocery shopping. She had put it off for as long as she could.

Barbie finally dried her tears and directed her sad-eyed gaze out the car window as they drove down the road, munching on hamburgers and sharing a large order of fries. Music filtered through the car, a rock station that played a few more oldies than the new stuff around. Barbie didn't seem to mind and even hummed along with one or two songs. For the moment, her terror was at bay.

As Elizabeth pulled into her driveway, Barbie finished her last bite of hamburger. It was dark now, a late fall evening with a chill in the air. Elizabeth felt herself break out in goose bumps as she opened the car door. "Let's get inside and have a cup of hot cocoa."

"Sounds wonderful," Barbie murmured, giving a light shiver. Her eyes darted from the porched, one-story houses of the modest Atlanta neighborhood to the old elms and maples that marched like soldiers down the side of the road, forming a canopy over it. Brilliantly colored leaves lushly carpeted the street and Elizabeth's small lawn. She'd have to hire someone to rake and mow this week. She'd put it on her to-do list, along with two hundred other items....

She dropped her purse on the small table just inside the front door. "Do you have homework, Barbie?"

"Some, not much. But I'm not sure I'm up to concentrating right now." Her mood was changing again.

"Sure you are," Elizabeth answered in a no-nonsense voice. "I have some chores to do before I can relax a little. Why don't you sit at the kitchen table and get your homework done while I do my stuff? Then, if you want a shower, I'll get you a big T-shirt and a toothbrush."

The young girl's hint of a smile disappeared as quickly as it came. "That sounds great."

"Fine. I'll put some stuff for you on the guest room bed. That's the second door on the right," she said, motioning down the hall.

Without looking back, Elizabeth went to her bedroom. She needed a respite from so much tension and emotion. From the look on Barbie's face, the teenager needed some private time, too.

Reaching into the closet, Elizabeth pulled out

one of several large T-shirts. From the bathroom, she snatched a cheap toothbrush still in its wrapper, and then, as an afterthought, grabbed an old pink chenille robe and took it to the guest bedroom.

It wasn't a particularly luxurious room, but it was homey and in good taste. Twin beds dressed in black-and-tan checks had their headboards against one wall, while a dresser and an old-fashioned dressing table and bench sat opposite. A sisal rug decorated the floor, black-and-tan-checked curtains over sheers over miniblinds hung at the one large window. Instead of prints or paintings, there were several photos, both black-and-white and color, mounted between sheets of glass. They accented the walls, interrupted occasionally with other photos in old frames that had been bought from garage sales and painted in various jewel-toned colors.

While Barbie completed her homework, Elizabeth took a quick shower and put on an oversize T-shirt and a pair of comfortable bike shorts— her uniform when she was home alone. That, along with an afghan and a good TV show that made her think and laugh, was her idea of heaven.

As she came into the kitchen, Barbie was closing her history book. "Done," the girl said. "What's next?"

"Take your shower and I'll fix us some cocoa," Elizabeth promised.

Fifteen minutes later, they were seated in opposite corners of the couch, sharing a block-patterned afghan knit from multiple shades of white, tan and green wool.

Barbie looked as if she was right at home, sipping her cocoa and laughing at some of the stories she told of her childhood. Elizabeth felt a little relieved. She'd gotten the impression that Barbie's dad was some sort of an ogre. Instead, it sounded as if he tried so hard to be a part of his daughter's life that he was bordering on intruding into her privacy and thoughts.

"...And then he told me that if I was going to run away, it was all right with him, but I wasn't allowed to cross the street."

Elizabeth laughed. "And what did you say to that?"

"I told him that was fine. I knew that Mom would help me if I needed it. But meanwhile, I stopped shaking in my patent leathers, 'cause I knew that Mom had put him up to following me. I was afraid Daddy might take me across the street to the schoolyard and I wouldn't have a way to get back home. That was what had started my rebellion to begin with. I had wanted to play there and Mom had said no."

It was time to focus the conversation on the present. "You miss your mom a bunch, don't you?"

Barbie tried not to let her eyes tear up. Instead, she stared at the cup of cocoa and spoke slowly, letting Elizabeth know she'd given that question some thought. "I miss her so much. When she died, much of the laughter in our household left. She was the glue that kept me safe and held us together as a family, you know?" Barbie glanced up, then back down quickly. "Mom had an answer or an explanation for everything. I never felt alone when she was alive, even when she was really, really sick."

"Do you feel alone now?"

"All the time." She closed her eyes for a moment. "At least I did until I met...my baby's father."

Good. She was realizing that this situation involved an actual baby, not some *thing*—thinking that would allow her to keep the problem at bay. Elizabeth decided not to broach the subject of the father yet. "Have you told your dad this?"

Barbie gave a short laugh. "His answer is that he's my dad and I shouldn't feel alone. He's there for me." She looked up at Elizabeth, begging her to understand. "But when I try to talk to him about boys or periods or other things, he gets all flustered and tells me that boys are nothing but walking hormones and that my mom left me a tape on girls' periods, and maybe I should listen to it again."

Elizabeth took Barbie's cup and poured her a little more cocoa from a cozy-covered teapot, then handed it back to her without saying anything.

"But I can't." Barbie's anguish was apparent in her every movement.

"Why?"

"Because I hear her voice and know she was dying when she said all that stuff. She was trying to cram all the advice she thought I'd need to know to be an adult onto those tapes before she left. It hurts to hear it!"

Barbie began crying as if her heart was shattering into thousands of pieces. Elizabeth reached for her, allowing her own tears to fall. She wasn't sure if she was crying for the girl in her arms or the young, naive girl inside herself.

Loss of a loved one was so difficult for adults to cope with. It was harder for a child, who saw other, more complete families and wanted the same.

It took several minutes before Barbie finally pulled back and gave Elizabeth a watery smile. "Thanks, Miss Gallagher."

"Call me Elizabeth, okay?"

They both gave a low chuckle, dispelling the awkwardness of the moment.

Elizabeth wasn't prepared when the doorbell rang, but after she looked through the peephole, she steeled herself for a confrontation with the man on the other side. It was obviously Barbie's father. He looked exhausted and angry. He'd taken off his suit jacket and was wearing the vest, dress shirt and pants of an expensive three-piece suit. His rich, dark hair gleamed in the porch light; his even darker eyes were drawn and tired. A proud jaw and a nose that looked as if it had once been broken added to his intense good looks. His aggressive attitude was obvious as he stared back at the peephole, obviously guessing correctly that she was giving him the once-over.

When Elizabeth opened the door, he looked surprised in turn. His eyes widened and darted up to the brass numbers just below the porch light. "Uh, Miss Gallagher?" His gaze dropped down her bare legs, then rose to find the outline of her breasts inside the oversize but thin T-shirt.

She recognized his voice from their phone conversation earlier in the week. "Yes. Mr. Damati?"

"Yes." His voice hardened. "My staff looked up your home address for me and I decided to come right over instead of paging you. I hope that's all right."

She refused to sanction his ignoring her instructions. "I guess it had better be, since it's a fait accompli."

"Is my daughter here?" He looked past her into the room, finally spying Barbie curled up in the corner of the couch. The look of relief and love that washed over his face for a brief moment eased any fears Elizabeth might have had. "Baby?"

"Hi, Daddy," Barbie said, her voice low and a touch resentful. "I thought you had that important meeting and couldn't be disturbed."

Barbie's father walked through the door Elizabeth held open and went straight to the couch, placing a light kiss on the top of his daughter's head. "I explained to you just how important that meeting was to our future, baby. I tried to change it, but it couldn't be held any other time."

"I know," she said, pleating the afghan covering her legs instead of looking at him. "You didn't come here to take me home did you?"

"Yes."

She stared up at him, dismay in her gaze. "I don't want to go home yet, Dad. I'm not ready!" Her tears began again.

His impatience was immediately apparent.

"What's there to get ready for? You don't even have to dress. It's fifteen minutes away."

Barbie's tears continued to flow.

He looked completely confused. "Now what did I say?"

"I'm not ready to go home yet!" she cried before scooting off the couch and running down the hall to the guest bedroom. "You just ruined everything, Daddy!"

"Barbie!" he demanded. "Come back here!"

Elizabeth closed the front door and walked to his side. "She's upset with the world right now. It has nothing to do with you."

He frowned. "How do you know? You've had only one session with her, and I wasn't there to smooth the way."

Elizabeth raised a brow. "I'm a psychologist and a woman. Besides that, I've talked to your daughter half the afternoon and all this evening."

He gave her a long stare before he finally relented and heaved a sigh. "I'm sorry. I'm just frustrated." He ran a hand around his neck as if to ease the strain. "I've talked to her every day of her life and I still can't tell whether she's hurt, frustrated, angry with me or just plain *angry*."

Elizabeth almost felt sorry for him. "Pregnancy is making her emotions unstable right now. Her present problems look overwhelming to her."

"*Her* present problems? Seems to me it's everyone's problem, including the young boy who...did this."

"The 'dastardly deed'?"

He shrugged, as if he didn't care what her opinion was. "If you want to call it that."

"Mr. Damati, this wasn't an immaculate conception. The deed was accomplished by two. According to your daughter, it wasn't rape, so I have to assume that she agreed to having sex. That makes her a party to her own condition."

He glared. "Are you letting some sexed-up twerp off scot-free?"

"No." She looked him straight in the eye, not batting an eyelash. "Are you giving him *all* the credit for Barbie's pregnancy?"

He glared back, brown eyes flashing. But slowly, his anger waned enough for him to unbend. "No. Not all."

"Well, at least we agree on something," she said calmly, even though her insides were clenched tighter than a fist. She took a deep breath and privately wished she hadn't dressed so casually. It was hard to be dignified in an oversize, very faded T-shirt. "Why don't you talk to her?" she suggested. "Second door on the right."

He gave a quick smile. "Thanks."

"No problem. I'll be in my room across the hall," she told him, as much to assure his privacy with his daughter as to let him know she was nearby.

Barbie's father followed Elizabeth around the corner, then knocked on the closed door. When his daughter called a watery "Come in," he did just that, but not before giving Elizabeth a nod of thanks.

She slipped into her own room, closed the

door and gave a sigh. Barbie's father was one strong character; Elizabeth felt as if he'd sucked all the air out of the house.

It was a good thing she was a dyed-in-the-wool career woman committed to staying single. Barbie's father could change a nun into a mother with just his smile. At least Elizabeth suspected so—she had yet to see his full smile.

And that was a silly thing to think, considering the circumstances facing his daughter, who had probably succumbed to a similar smile.

Elizabeth turned on the small bedside lamp and sat down in her wicker rocker. Draping her hands on the arms, she closed her eyes and rocked back and forth, soothing her frayed emotions. She tried to relax by focusing on anything except the problems that awaited her outside her bedroom door.

The room was monochromatic in tone, with pale peach walls and matching curtains and comforter, and goose down pillows stacked against the washed-oak headboard. A thick white Berber carpet accented the floor. The room was feminine and easy to maintain, and as relaxing as Elizabeth could make it. She loved it, enjoying the peace it seemed to give to her ruffled soul. In fact, she couldn't count the hours she'd spent in this rocker, rocking away the tension of the day, the week, the month. The problems.

And here she was, doing it again.

A knock on the door brought her back to the present and her guests in the other room. "Come in."

The door opened a crack and Barbie's father

called, "Miss Gallagher?" His thick-lashed dark eyes darted around the room, taking in the decor. His eyes widened. "Quite an interesting room."

Elizabeth's laugh was relaxed and easy now that she'd had a few moments to herself. "I've found that *interesting* is one of those words that hide a lot of truths. Are you studying to be a diplomat?"

He looked innocent, even though she knew by his eyes that he felt like smiling, too. "Not in this life." His expression changed to one more somber. "May I speak with you a moment?"

"Of course." She stood and walked toward the door, unwilling to allow him into her sanctuary and upset it with his energy. "How about a cup of tea?" Without waiting for his answer, Elizabeth squeezed by him and headed toward the kitchen. She caught a whiff of his aftershave as she brushed by. It was a light spice scent that seemed rich and sexy at the same time.

Not that she was interested.

When the tea was ready, she and Barbie's father sat in the small kitchen nook and quietly stared out the moonlit window as they collected their thoughts. She was surprised that it didn't feel awkward.

He finally broke the companionable silence. "Barbie seems to think she should stay with you tonight."

He was due an explanation, she thought. "It's not my usual practice to bring home clients, Mr. Damati. But when she said you weren't home, I knew I couldn't drop her off at your house and leave her alone. She's sixteen physically, but emotionally right now, she's only about ten years old. Everything looks topsy-turvy."

He pinched the bridge of his nose. "I know. Did she say what she was upset about?"

Elizabeth raised a brow. "Her life changes, perhaps?" she stated dryly.

"Sorry. I mean did something else just happen that made her cry?"

"Hormones and the circumstances that are forcing her into making decisions she's not prepared for."

Ben Damati looked so hurt Elizabeth wanted to comfort him. But she didn't.

"Then why doesn't she turn to me?" he asked. "I've been home every night for weeks, except tonight. Why would she turn to you? She's only visited your office once."

Obviously he didn't realize he'd just insulted her. Elizabeth let it slide. "My guess is that she's hungry for female company."

"She has female friends. She has her grandmother, who comes to visit often. Her mom's sister comes into town once every two or three months. And she's never farther away than a phone call. Barbie's never at a loss for women."

"She's looking for a mother figure, Mr. Damati." Elizabeth cocked her head and gazed at him. "Barbie says that her mother died when she was eleven. Have you never thought of marrying again?"

His defensiveness returned and he looked at her as if she were one step up from a dolt. "I'll do anything I can for my daughter, except ruin my own life. Marriage is where I draw the line. I'm not about to take up with a woman just because Barbie needs someone for the next few years. I'd be stuck in a marriage long after she left home."

"I wasn't suggesting you marry for your daughter. I just thought you might have met someone and decided *not* to marry because of Barbie."

He hesitated a long moment. "No, there's no one in my life now."

"What a shame."

"Enough!" He held up a hand. "I'm not arguing whether or not I should have married for my daughter's sake. I'm not married, and we have this problem. Let's start from where we are."

She gave him a level gaze and a nod. He was right, but her curiosity was piqued. "Your daughter is starving for some kind of mother figure in her life. I know you care, but at this point she needs masculine appreciation and female conversation." Elizabeth decided not to pull her punches now. "Obviously, you're a very busy man and, she's a teenager who needs more attention than she's getting. If this situation is going to ease for the two of you, you might find a substitute woman who can act as a role model."

His frustration and anger were more than apparent. "So this is all *my* fault? Some hormonal, snot-nosed boy comes along and makes a mess out of my daughter's life, and I'm the one who takes the fall, is that it?"

"No," Elizabeth corrected. "It's Barbie who's taking the fall. We're just bystanders. Although you're hurt, you don't have to live with the life-changing consequences of any decision Barbie makes right now. *She* does. For the rest of her life."

Her words must have struck home like a battering ram. The breath went out of his lungs in a whoosh. He ran a hand over his forehead and eyes as if to wipe away the thought she'd just planted. It didn't work. "Damn," he muttered in a low tone.

"I'm sorry if I sounded as if I was browbeating you Mr. Damati. I'm not. I'm just showing you another side to this problem." She reached out and covered his hand with hers to give comfort. Slowly the stiffness left him, and he turned his palm over to enclose her fingers. "Now we can move on to solving the problem at hand. Namely, helping Barbie make a decision about this baby that she can live with."

He gave Elizabeth a searching look, a wry smile framing his mouth. "Where did you learn such a no-nonsense approach? In college?"

"No, much earlier than that." She withdrew her hand and stood. "But that's another story. Right now, I'd better check on Barbie and see how she's doing."

He stood up, too, looking as tired as she felt. "She wants to stay here for the night. Is that okay?"

"Of course. I invited her earlier. Is that okay with you, Mr. Damati?"

"Call me Ben, and it's fine with me. I'll be home when she returns from school tomorrow afternoon."

"Good." Elizabeth stood and, with as much dignity as she could manage in bike pants, walked him toward the door. "Let's just take this one day at a time while we help Barbie figure out what to do. Your school district has a special class that pregnant girls can attend, if she wants to do that."

He looked stunned, his dark eyes widening. "Are there that many?"

She opened the front door. "Enough. Most school districts have them. Just because she attends a private school doesn't mean the options aren't available. But we'll discuss that another time, too."

"Thank you for being here for her. I guess I'm just having a hard time adapting to this. Barbie's been my whole life focus for so long, it's hard to imagine her old enough for this problem, let alone knee deep into it." His expression turned hard and cold. "I'd like to punch someone's lights out for this, but she won't even tell me who it is."

Elizabeth swayed a little, too tired to hide it. "Ben, can we discuss this some other time? I'm dead on my feet and have to get some sleep."

"Of course. May I call you later this week?"

"Please. Barbie has my number if you've lost it."

"Good night, Ms. Gallagher. And thank you."

"Good night, Mr. Damati. And you're welcome."

Closing the door behind him, Elizabeth headed back to her room, turning out the lights as she went. One minute later she was in bed asleep, everything forgotten.

But sometime during the night, she turned over and woke up enough to remember the rich, brown depth of Ben Damati's eyes.

Just before falling asleep again, she smiled.

2

As soon as Elizabeth hit the snooze alarm, she heard the distinct clamor of Barbie in the bathroom. Morning sickness.

Muttering under her breath, she joined her young charge. Barbie looked so pitiful curled against the wall next to the commode, arms crossed over her almost-flat tummy. Her skin was a light shade of green.

Elizabeth sat on the edge of the tub and stroked Barbie's hair away from her face. "Bad morning?"

"It's happened every morning for the past month. It'll stop in just a minute or so," Barbie said, her tone sounding as dejected as she looked.

"It should stop completely in another month or so."

"I thought it was supposed to stop by now." Tension in the young girl's voice underlined her fears.

"For some," Elizabeth said reassuringly. "It varies for everyone, honey."

Barbie closed her eyes and swallowed a few times. "I hope I'm through soon." She looked so young and vulnerable—just like the child she was. "It's not fun."

"You're doing just fine." Elizabeth wet a washcloth, then handed it to Barbie.

Wordlessly, she wiped her face. After taking a deep breath, she looked up at Elizabeth. Her blue eyes were wide and filled with frustration. "Why don't men carry babies and go through all this? Was God mad at us?"

Elizabeth couldn't help the smile that tilted her mouth. "God was so thrilled with women that She gave childbearing to the gender She knew would take the best care. That's us."

Barbie stared at her a moment. "You're funny."

"And you're going to be late if you don't start getting ready now."

"Thanks."

Fifteen minutes later, Elizabeth had showered, curled the ends of her reddish brown hair and begun the process of putting on a touch of makeup.

The doorbell rang. Slipping a blue jersey dress over her head, she marched to the door in her stocking feet. But she felt her smile all the way to the tips of her toes when she opened the door to see Ben Damati.

"Beware of Italians bearing pastries," he warned in his rich baritone voice, but his engaging grin matched hers. "Is this an awkward time?"

"No," she assured him, getting the warm fuzzies just looking at him. For a second, she wondered why she'd be so attracted to a man who was so obviously out of her league. "Barbie's getting dressed now. Pour yourself a cup of coffee and we'll join you in just a few minutes."

"Take your time."

Elizabeth hurried down the hallway to the guest bedroom and stuck her head in the partially opened door. "Barbie?" The young girl was standing close to the mirror as she painstakingly applied lip gloss. "How are you feeling?"

She grimaced and dropped the lip gloss into her purse. "I feel like I've just been dragged through a knothole."

"I can imagine," Elizabeth said, coming into the room. She placed a hand on Barbie's slight shoulder. "Your dad's here with doughnuts."

Barbie gave a shudder. "Grease. Ugh." She looked at Elizabeth hopefully. "Do you have any bagels?"

"Yes." Impulsively, she gave Barbie's cheek a kiss, surprising both of them. "I'll keep your dad company in the kitchen."

As Elizabeth left the room, she took a deep breath. Tension flowed through her like hot lava. Was it due to Barbie's visit in her home or the handsome man standing in her kitchen?

She walked into the kitchen and poured herself a cup of coffee. "Did you make yourself at home?" she asked over her shoulder, not willing to look at him just yet. He might see the pleasure in her gaze.

"Yes, thanks. Did you tell Barbie I'm here?"

"Of course, but she wasn't too thrilled with your choice of breakfast pastry. Grease isn't sitting well in her tummy these days." Elizabeth walked over to the box sitting on the table. After choosing a chocolate covered doughnut for herself, she held it up as a salute to his good taste. "However, I don't have that problem, so I'll sacrifice myself and help you out."

Her humor went over his head. Ben looked stricken. "Dear God, I forgot about morning sickness."

"It happens to lots of women, Mr.—Ben."

"It happened to her mother—every morning for about five months." His brow creased. "But Barbie never said a word. She's just a kid, not a full-grown woman."

Elizabeth's eyes locked with his. He was pleading with her to tell him everything was all right. It wasn't.

"Tell that to the baby."

He looked startled.

Elizabeth softened. "She's old enough to carry a baby and young enough to be scared and in need of her father."

He closed his eyes. "I know."

"Sorry. I spoke out of turn."

His dark, sexy eyes opened and delved into hers. "What can I do? Help me. I'm so damn lost...."

Instead of thinking of the teenager in the other room, she wanted to hug the man. He was so scared he looked like a little boy. Her breath caught in her throat. "Relax. She needs you, she wants you in her life. She just needs females more right now."

"What happened to equality? Aren't men people, too?" he asked, trying to joke, but his pain was clear to see.

"Come on, women aren't that different from men." She smiled reassuringly. "Aren't you relieved to be with other men and not have to talk about feelings and emotions? Isn't it easier talking about sports than worrying about not hurting each other's feelings?"

His look said it all. Obviously, he liked that idea a lot.

"Well, women have their own language, too. That's why Barbie needs emotional support from another woman who's been there."

He was silent a long time. "I'm frustrated with this whole thing, and there's nothing I can do to relieve it." His fingers clenched around the coffee cup. "I'd still like to beat the hell out of the boy who did this."

The floor creaked and Elizabeth turned around. For the first time since she'd walked into the kitchen, she found herself distracted enough to look away. Ben was a powerful man, his charisma filling any room he entered.

"Hi, Daddy," Barbie said from the doorway. Ben looked up. She was the model of the perfect young lady, with her blond hair brushed till it shone, one side held in place with a small gold barrette. Her cobalt blue skirt and sweater hugged her youthful figure. She didn't look four months pregnant, but there was a small, definite bulge to her tummy. And she looked one step away from panic.

"Hey, baby, come sit down and have a doughnut," Ben coaxed. It was obvious that, to him, Barbie wasn't any older than ten or twelve.

"No doughnuts, Daddy." Barbie looked

pleadingly at Elizabeth. "Do you have that bagel?"

"Course," she replied, reaching for the butter. She'd already put a bagel in the toaster.

Barbie gave a quick smile, then slid into the seat next to her father.

"What's your next test, honey?" Ben asked, obviously searching for a topic that wasn't too controversial.

"Home ec. Friday."

The toaster popped up and Elizabeth placed the bagel on a plate and handed it to Barbie.

Ben's brows rose. "My favorite class."

"Home ec?" Elizabeth and Barbie said together.

"Sure." He grinned. "It was my favorite subject. Me and twenty-two girls. I didn't learn how to cook full meals, but I now realize how hard it is to make biscuits and cakes."

Elizabeth laughed.

Barbie looked shocked. "You did that just to be close to *girls?*"

"Yes." Ben nodded, a twinkle in his dark eyes. "I was seventeen and thought God had made girls just for me to enjoy." His face took on a wickedly wonderful expression. "Why do you think I kept warning you about boys? I was one that mothers warned their daughters about."

"You sound proud," Barbie said in a disgusted tone only a teenager could use. "If it had been a girl acting that way, she would have been called names not fit to mention in any company." She took a healthy bite of her bagel.

Her father had the grace to look guilty. "I

know there's a double standard. I'm not responsible for it."

"Neither am I," she said pointedly, taking another bite. Then the fight left her and her shoulders slumped. She stood, her back ramrod straight. "Excuse me, but I've got to finish getting ready for school."

After she left the room, Ben put his head in his hands for a moment. "No matter what I say, it's wrong."

Elizabeth smiled. "Remember the girls in home ec?"

Ben nodded.

"Well, your daughter is just like them. She's the same age and the same frame of mind."

"They were older for their years than Barbie," he protested, brushing off her suggestion.

"You were just younger."

He looked a little shocked. "Are you telling me it's payback time?"

Elizabeth stood, collecting napkins and placing cups in the sink. "This isn't about you, it's about Barbie."

He rubbed the back of his neck as if that would rub away the problems. "I'm completely out of my element. Give me a product to sell or a rendering to complete, and I know what to do. But when it comes to my daughter's well-being, I can't come up with a solution."

"Give her time. She'll find her own solutions. After all, you raised her."

"You mean, stay out of it?"

Elizabeth shrugged. "Not exactly. Help her

make those decisions that affect her. Don't take over."

"Like helping her figure out what the next step should be?"

"Exactly. Not *making* the next decision for her."

Ben grinned. His dark brown eyes bored into Elizabeth's and she felt the intimate warmth of his direct gaze. She was instantly captured by a smile that promised unspoken treats. For a moment she pitied the girls in that long-ago home ec class. They probably hadn't stood a chance, and she was sure he'd known it—even then.

"How about helping me with a few minor problems?"

Her eyes narrowed as she deliberately made herself impervious to his charm. "Anything above a hangnail is chargeable."

"How about dealing with a family wedding?"

"What's your definition of 'dealing'?"

Ben stared into his coffee cup for a moment, obviously not seeing it. He had a strong face, made handsome by rugged lines and angles. But it was his obvious sense of self, that confidence and charisma coupled with a hint of vulnerability, that made him irresistible.

He was a magnet for women if there ever was one.

His words caught her attention again. "...I mean, should I take Barbie and pretend everything's fine?"

Elizabeth was caught off guard for a moment, having lost track of the conversation. She cleared her throat. "I don't think a family wedding is the time to announce a pregnancy, especially if it isn't the bride's." At his frown, she grinned and patted his hand. "Take it easy. It was a joke."

But the handsome man had a one-track mind and he wasn't in a joking mood. "Should I take a date?"

Her heart jumped at the thought. She tamped that reaction down immediately. "Are you currently dating someone?"

"No."

She hated to admit how good that word sounded. If he was free... But that wasn't to be thought of now. She was supposed to be sensible. "Then this isn't the time to invite someone new."

His eyes locked with hers, the intensity of his dark-eyed gaze making her feel like squirming. His mouth gave a quirk she took to be a smile. She was staring at the sexy indentations on either side of his mouth when Ben's next words fell like tiny explosions. "Will you go with us? Please?"

She shook her head to clear it. "Go where?"

"To the wedding." He smiled again and his stern look dissolved. "With us."

"Oh, I couldn't. No," she said, shaking her head while effervescent champagne bubbles raced through her bloodstream. "No, not me." The bubbles kept coming.

"Why not?" he asked, capturing her hand. His thumb soothed the center of her palm sensuously. Whether he was doing this unconsciously or on purpose didn't matter. The effect was the same. "Are you involved with someone?"

"No. But that's not the point."

He looked smug as he continued. "Do you have an illness that would prevent you from dancing or talking to people you don't know and probably won't meet again?" he probed. Those slash marks on either side of his sexy mouth turned into heavy dimples now.

"No, of course not." She shook her head, but the bubbles of anticipation were floating to the surface. "But that's not the point, either."

"Are you allergic to light conversation, food, drinks or wedding cake?"

Elizabeth laughed. "No," she drawled, recognizing what was going to happen.

"Are you allergic to fathers or teenagers? Or sunny Sunday afternoons in a parklike setting where a bride, a groom and a whole lot of guests seem happy and carefree, if only for a little while?"

"Of course not."

His thumb moved, caressing the top of her hand, feeling the fine bones there and stroking them as if they were porcelain. "Then please say yes. I promise to be the best of hosts."

"I know, but..."

"I'll be on my best behavior." His brows rose. "Please?"

"It's not right. I can't help Barbie and date you."

"Then don't consider it a date. Consider it helping Barbie and getting stuck with her staid old father."

"I don't know," she said, still shaking her head, but her gaze was searching his for...what?

It was only a wedding, she told herself. She wasn't making a commitment for life to the man.

"And you can send me a bill for your services."

Her gaze narrowed. "What services?"

"Psychology. Isn't that what you do?"

She relaxed. "Thank you for remembering, but weddings aren't usually covered."

"I don't care." He grinned and showed those dimples again, warming her heart. "Send me the bill anyway."

"I don't..." she began. The man was like a steamroller, flattening every objection she had.

Barbie came into the kitchen, her arms full of books and her long face practically dragging on the floor. It was true she had problems, but it was also apparent that there was just a touch of Sarah Bernhardt in her. "I'm ready for school," she said in a low monotone.

Elizabeth slipped her hand from under Ben's and stood up. She looked at Barbie, then back to Ben. "Fine, Barbie, I'll meet you in the car, okay?"

Barbie nodded and walked out of the kitchen toward the front door. "Bye, Dad. See you tonight."

Ben stood and watched her leave. "Bye, Barbie. I love you."

There was no answer.

Elizabeth made her decision. No man needed to be punished for his wife's death, and yet, from Elizabeth's point of view, that was exactly what Barbie was doing. "Yes. I'll go."

Ben turned toward her, his dark eyes alight

with relief. "I'm so glad. Thank you." He leaned forward and placed a chaste kiss on her cheek. "You'll enjoy it. I promise."

Where his lips touched her cheek, there was heat. The rest of her skin seemed chilled by comparison. Her smile was spontaneous and heartfelt. "You're very welcome. Call me later in the day and leave the particulars on my answering machine."

"I'll call this evening and speak to you personally," he replied with just the right amount of force.

"Very well. But now I've got to go. And if I have to go, so do you, Mr. Damati." Elizabeth tried to keep her mind on what she was doing, but somehow her thoughts were scattered.

"Ben," he corrected, reaching in his pocket for keys as they walked to the door.

"Ben," she repeated with a laugh.

"Goodbye," he said simply, but the look in his eyes said something else that heated her through and through. It promised one hell of a hello when next they met.

3

HE WAS A MAN with a problem. She didn't have to embellish on that.

It wasn't his fault he was good-looking. Elizabeth doubted that looks had much to do with his basic ideals, or the way he saw the world. He was just a man. Genes gave him a handsome face, a great build and intelligence, but his looks had no bearing on what type of man he'd grown into. Well, she amended, not much anyway.

It took almost two hours to go through the grocery store and pick and choose what she wanted: fresh, cheap and quick to cook was a tall order. And to top it off, she hated shopping at the end of the workday, with everyone else, but that was her own fault. She could have shopped on the weekend, when she'd had more time. Instead, she had puttered around the house, loath to leave it for the world outside. She'd cleaned out closets and weeded flower beds as if anticipating a visit from a fictitious, all-important mother-in-law.

Not that she would put up with that sort of thing. No, siree. Oh, no, not her...

A few years ago, Elizabeth had decided she would always be single. Many women her age had or did live with someone, but not Elizabeth. She wouldn't make herself that vulnerable to another's whims. Besides, she enjoyed her privacy. She liked coming home and kicking off her shoes and padding around. If she wanted cereal for dinner, that was all right too.

At the no-longer-tender age of thirty, she'd realized one essential fact about herself—she was too easily influenced by those she liked. The cure was to stay away from people who could sway her before she knew what she wanted. That way, she couldn't be talked into doing things she didn't want to do. She stood on her own two feet, doing what she believed was important work and, two days a week ignored all but emergencies in her private practice to take referrals from the school district, helping unwed mothers or mothers-to-be with their problems. It was the most gratifying service she'd ever performed, actively contributing to the happiness and emotional health of so many young women.

Elizabeth loved her work. The intangible rewards were great, even though that didn't pay for an unexpected house or car repair. What she earned from the school district was pitiful. The hours were long.

That didn't mean she couldn't go out once in a while, however. She *was* human, after all. She needed adult conversation—with males—as much as the next woman. And her work partners didn't allow her to vegetate. Marina and Jamie kept telling her that just because she wasn't in the market for a long-term affair didn't mean she couldn't have a social life.

Which brought her to her immediate problem. If she was going to a wedding with Barbie and her handsome father, she'd better find something to wear. A quick look through her closet had told her it was splurge time. She'd have to go shopping in the next few days.

She liked that idea. Ignoring the fact that she enjoyed being with Ben Damati more than she cared to admit, she pretended it was to make an impression on his family.

Picking up the recorder in the seat next to her, she flipped the button and began speaking. "Remind me to ask Marina to take over Barbie Damati's case." She clicked if off.

When she drove up to her house, she noticed that the front storm door was ajar. That wasn't normal. Brushing it off as someone delivering junk mail or selling door-to-door, she grabbed several plastic grocery bags and walked around to the back door. She stopped still.

On the large welcome mat, Barbie was curled on her side, arms wrapped around her knees. Her eyes were closed, her head resting on a leather backpack.

Elizabeth rearranged the grocery bags cutting into her palms and bent over the young girl. "Barbie? Wake up, darlin', and open the door for me."

The young girl blinked several times before she suddenly shot up. "Oh, hey, I'm so sorry!" she said, brushing back her thick blond hair. "I'm just so sleepy lately," she explained breathlessly as she reached for the keys in Elizabeth's white fingers and unlocked the door. Although her bright blue eyes were dry, Barbie's cheeks showed the ravages of recent tears.

Elizabeth decided on the direct approach. "That's normal, dear, as I'm sure you're finding out." She dropped her plastic bags on the kitchen table. "Grab some of the bags in the back of the car, will you? We'll get them in and then you can tell me what's going on while we put the food away."

Barbie did as she was told, running out to the car and returning with as many grocery bags as she could carry.

If only Elizabeth felt that energy right now, instead of craving to sit down amd watch some mindless comedy on television, vegging out for a while.

"How come you know so much about pregnancy? Have you ever been? Pregnant, I mean?" Barbie asked a little later as they emptied the bags and put the groceries away.

"Never been pregnant. Never jumped off a bridge before, either. Doesn't mean I don't know what it's like and what the results will be." Elizabeth smiled to lessen the sting of her words. "I've studied it, though, and I've got many close friends who can bore you for hours with anything and everything you ever wanted to know."

"Kinda like shop talk?"

"Kinda. Now tell me what's on your mind." Elizabeth began heating water for tea. "Why were you sleeping on my doorstep?"

The young girl made a face, but her eyes glazing with tears gave away the importance of the visit. "Do we have to talk about it now?"

"I think I'm due an explanation." Elizabeth's tone was soft, but firm. "Don't you? You've spent the night here, which is against every rule, and now I find you here again. What's up?"

"I'll go," Barbie said, her voice the same monotone she'd used this morning.

"If you want," Elizabeth said calmly. "But there was obviously a reason you came here. Don't you think it would be better if you talked about what's on your mind?"

Barbie's eyes teared up. "The baby's on my mind every minute. I don't know what to do, who to turn to. Everybody's got an opinion and I don't know which one is right!" She began crying in earnest.

Elizabeth put her arm around Barbie's shoulders and led her to a kitchen chair. Then she sat next to her, facing her and holding her hands. "Look, you're right when you say there are lots of problems you have to face. But don't let them overwhelm you. Take one problem at a time and solve it. Then take the next one and the next one. That way, they'll be manageable and it will work out. I promise."

"Yes." Barbie gave a hiccup. "But I want it to work out in my favor, not someone else's!"

"Anyone else in particular?"

"Yes!" she cried. "How come I'm stuck with being pregnant and *he* can walk around as if he hasn't got a care in the world? How come his friends tell him what a *stud* he is and I'm lower than a—a snake's belly!" she shouted. Hurt and anguish shone in her youthful eyes. "How come?" she whispered. "How come?"

"Oh, Barbie," Elizabeth crooned, her thumbs soothing the top of her clenched hands. "Life's *not* fair, but here we are, anyway. Who knows why some people have a conscience and some don't? Some guys don't have a clue how to nurture or make peace, or to keep a family together. And if they're not raised that way, they can't seem to figure it out for themselves. They have to be taught. But not all guys are alike."

"Well, from where I'm sitting, it sure looks like it." She sniffled. "So it's up to me to make all the decisions, because he refuses to admit to anything. He told me his parents said he doesn't have to own up to anyone." She grew teary again. "They told him that I probably slept around and am just pointing fingers. That it's my problem."

Elizabeth hurt for the young girl. But she'd heard it all before. This boy wasn't from the first family to use that excuse. "That's right. It's your problem and your choice as long as you choose to protect him."

"I don't want to protect him! I don't want him in my life at all!" she cried, but the high-pitched denial didn't quite ring true.

"If you decide to keep the baby, the father has a right to be part of your child's life, whether you like it or not. And so do the fraternal grandparents. There are laws to that effect. All babies need as much family as they can get, including aunts, uncles and grandparents. It's called a support base and we all do better that way."

"I only have Dad in my corner, and I didn't turn out so bad," she objected. Then she glanced down at their locked hands before looking back up. Her tear-filled eyes widened in dawning comprehension. "I *did* turn out badly, didn't I?"

"Don't even go there, Barbie," Elizabeth admonished. "Pregnancy out of wedlock is a mistake, but don't mix it up with being a bad person. If that was the case, half the world would be bad."

"I know, but—"

"No buts," Elizabeth stated firmly. "Everyone makes mistakes. If they don't, they're not living life, which is a mistake in itself. So that we don't repeat mistakes, we try to learn from them."

"Well, I'm learning from this one," Barbie promised, letting go of Elizabeth to wipe away the fresh tears trickling down her chin.

"Good. That's all you need to do, honey." Elizabeth stood. They'd had enough truth for the moment. "Now help me cook dinner and we'll talk some more. You still haven't told me why you're here. It wasn't because of the father of your child, was it?"

She busied herself with rattling pots and pans, hoping that Barbie would finally relax. The young girl reached for the large pot Elizabeth held out, then began filling it with hot water.

Carefully choosing three onions, Elizabeth began peeling them, but was interrupted by the doorbell. One look out her front window told her that Ben's sleek, maroon Jaguar was parked in her driveway.

"Get the door, will you?" she asked Barbie.

With a silent, downcast nod, the young girl did as she was told.

Elizabeth heard the soft sounds of conversation. Ben did most of the talking, but Barbie was answering. That was good. If she could ever get the girl to open up...

"Hi," Ben said as he stepped into the kitchen. He wore a dark blue, three-piece suit that fit as if it had been made for him, which it probably had. "We've got to keep meeting like this or we may not meet at all."

She laughed. His tone was teasing and yet not too familiar. He had a way about him that made Elizabeth want to be near him. Charisma, plain and simple. "You must not live far away," she said. "Otherwise I wouldn't see you this often."

"Not too far," he admitted. "But when I tried to find Barbie, one of her girlfriends said she was probably here. I decided to trot right over in case I missed any of the good stuff, like girl talk."

Barbie had the grace to flush. "I needed to talk to Miss Gallagher," she said defensively.

"About what, doll?"

"Don't call me doll!" Barbie protested. "Just because Mom named me after one doesn't mean I am. I'm real!"

For a moment, Ben stood perfectly still, appearing shocked at his daughter's tirade, then looked as if he was grasping for patience. "I know, honey. It's just a term of endearment. Nothing more."

"You say that, but I know better. You've always thought of me as a little toy," she repeated stubbornly. "But I'm a lot more than that."

Elizabeth focused on the onion in her hand, chopping it carefully while she listened. Their discussion wasn't about dolls, it was about Barbie's concept of herself.

"I never played with dolls, Barbie, so I can't really relate." His voice was low, but there was a hint of impatience seeping through.

Elizabeth decided it was time to step in before this escalated. "Barbie, would you please set that pan of water on the stove to heat?" she asked.

Barbie gave her dad one last glare, then nodded and completed her task.

Elizabeth knew there would be no vegetating in front of the TV and watching mindless programs tonight. "Have you eaten yet?" she asked Ben.

"No. But I don't want to burden you with my family problems. You'll never talk to me again if this keeps up." Again, his tone was teasing, but his eyes told her how serious he was.

She turned toward the stove. "Barbie was on my doorstep asleep, when I returned home. We're preparing dinner. You can join us or not, but Barbie's already involved with the process." Elizabeth tried to be nonchalant about dinner, but her heart beat a different rhythm. This wasn't a good TV night, anyway. *Let him stay. Let him stay. Let him stay.*

"What can I do to help?"

Why hadn't she checked her mascara and blush? *Don't bother thinking that, Elizabeth.* "Can you cook?" she asked.

"Of course," Ben said, slipping off his jacket and slinging it over a chair. Then he rolled up his crisp, white shirtsleeves to expose tanned and muscled forearms. "Do you have an apron?"

"Top drawer under the microwave." She pushed the remaining onions she'd chosen along with the chopping knife and wooden block toward the end of the counter without looking at him again. Her heart was racing already. "You can start here."

"Daddy hates chopping onions," Barbie volunteered as she returned to the kitchen. "He says his hands stink for days."

"And so they do," Elizabeth said. "Just about as long as hands smell like oil when you change your car's filter."

"Are you two picking on me?" he questioned, standing back from the onion as he began the cutting process. "Oil smells are manly. Onion is not."

"Oh really? What's manly about smelling like old oil?" Elizabeth asked, quirking a teasing brow in his direction. "And since when is onion a woman's smell? Better still, exactly what is manly?"

Distracted from moodiness, Barbie giggled. "Yeah, Daddy. What's manly?"

Ben took their teasing good-naturedly, not stopping his chopping. "Manly is anything that smells tough, looks heavy, might be dead and doesn't have embroidered flowers."

Both women giggled.

"Now you two," he said. "What's feminine?"

Elizabeth glanced at Barbie. The young girl looked thoughtful for a moment. "I'm not sure," she began, her gaze darting to Elizabeth for a clue.

"Think, Barbie," Elizabeth prompted. "What did we discuss the other day?"

The teenager looked at her, eyes narrowing speculatively. Suddenly she brightened. "Of course! Anything."

But Ben hadn't caught on. "Anything what?"

"That's it, Daddy. Feminine is anything we want it to be!"

"Good going!" Elizabeth chuckled, giving her young student a one-armed hug.

"Unfair."

"Not at all." Elizabeth dumped celery and tomatoes into the water and stirred. "It's right on target. We don't let things keep us from doing something just because it's not 'feminine'."

"I know, I know," Ben groaned. "Unlike us poor men, you get the job done. We just do our job."

Barbie laughed. "Now you tell me, Daddy. Where was all this hidden wisdom on males and females before now?" She gave Elizabeth a wink, which startled her. "Is it because Ms. Gallagher is here and you're trying to impress her?"

"No, munchkin," he said, tapping Barbie on the nose. "It's because you're listening to me right now, just as I'm listening to you." Ben raised a brow. "Maybe we're both learning something."

Barbie's smile slipped just a little. "Maybe."

Elizabeth stepped in. "And maybe you'd better throw in the hamburger, Barbie. We've got everything chopped. It's time to get this show on the road."

"Yes, ma'am," she said, working quickly and efficiently.

"I gather you've done this before," Elizabeth commented. "You're good."

Surprisingly, Barbie blushed at the compliment. "Thanks. Granny Linda used to let me help with spaghetti."

"And Barbie took cooking lessons from one of the better Atlanta chefs last summer." Ben's voice held a note of pride in his daughter.

"It shows."

While Elizabeth poured the remaining ingredients into the pot, Barbie searched through the utensil drawer looking for a wooden spoon.

"My dad used to say that it didn't matter what you cooked, it had to be stirred by a wooden spoon to be good." Ben took the spoon Barbie offered and began the stirring.

"Italian?"

"Very."

Elizabeth glanced over at Barbie. "I'm surprised Barbie is so fair."

"Ahh. Haven't you heard about us mean and nasty Romans conquering England and taking the women and children back to Rome as slaves? When we did, only the wealthy could afford to buy them. Consequently, many of the elite of Italy are blue eyed and blond haired."

"Daddy!" Barbie protested.

"So that's where Barbie got her hair color?"

"No, she got it from her maternal grandmother's side of the family. Norwegian descent.

But the story is still true,'' he stated without a bit of compunction. ''We Damatis just weren't part of the aristocracy. Besides, like many Americans, all we have left Italian is the name.''

Elizabeth grinned. She couldn't help but like him. He was sexy and his personality was magnetic. ''Well, I'll never tell,'' she said, earning another giggle from Barbie.

In the sizzling pot, herbs and spices blended together, their delicious scent wafting through the room.

''Add some basil,'' Elizabeth prompted.

Again Barbie did as she was told.

''Now we let it simmer.''

''And get the spaghetti ready?''

''Yes.''

''Well, if I've got to do the dirty work while you two have all the fun, then at least I can tell some jokes,'' Ben said, his tone teasing. ''Knock, knock.''

He told one joke after another, all silly and sweet and funny. Barbie groaned, letting Elizabeth know she'd heard many of them before. But Elizabeth hadn't. She laughed at them all....

Half an hour later, they sat down at the kitchen table and ate heartily. Ben had insisted on making garlic bread, and it was just right—crisp and toasty on the outside, soft and buttery on the inside.

Elizabeth found a dusty bottle of fairly good merlot that some date—she couldn't recall who—had brought over with his high hopes. Apparently, those hopes hadn't been realized or she would have remembered.

Barbie drank ice cold milk in a stemmed glass, grinning as if she was having the time of her life. Elizabeth laughed because she *was* having the time of her life. Her tiredness had disappeared, replaced by an easy sense of calm. And maybe just a zing of excitement.

She ignored the excitement part. That would mean acknowledging the fact that she was very attracted to Ben. No. No way. Not.

When she finished her last bite, Barbie gave a satisfied sigh and sat back, a white milk mustache outlining her top lip. "That was delicious."

"Thanks to you and your dad," Elizabeth said, quick to give credit where it was due. "It was a joint effort."

"No, this was different than how we make it. It's much better." She turned toward her father. "Isn't it, Daddy?"

"Yes." He tried to look crestfallen at her opinion. "But I didn't see the whole process, so I don't know if we can duplicate it." His dark eyes twinkled at Elizabeth, making her smile in return. "Unless, of course, we can find a way to make Ms. Gallagher talk. Or we could bring her over to the house whenever we want this dish again." Ben twirled a make-believe mustache.

Barbie giggled. "I'll disappear to watch TV and do my homework—and leave you to wrestle her recipes away from her."

"I'll call you in when it's time to clear up the kitchen." Ben's voice was casual.

Barbie quickly wiped her mouth and stood. "Okay."

Elizabeth suddenly felt awkward. Until now,

Barbie had been a buffer and the conversation had flowed easily. All at once Elizabeth wasn't sure what to say. She wished she had an ounce of her sister Mary's diplomacy. Or her sister Virginia's gift of the gab. But she didn't.

Direct and to the point was all she ever was. She decided to continue on the only path she knew: the direct one. "You're probably wondering why Barbie was here. I don't know why myself. Barbie was on my doorstep when I got home, like I said. I assumed you two had had an argument."

Ben shook his head, his smile gone, replaced by a puzzled expression that creased his forehead. She wanted to reach out and smooth the creases, ease them from his brow. Instead, she clasped her hands together tightly in her lap.

Ben shook his head. "Wasn't me. Must have been the other man in her life." The ease was gone. His voice was laced with tension.

"Sorry." She took a sip of her wine. "But I already crossed the line of professionalism when Barbie came home with me last night."

"That was my secretary's fault."

"It doesn't matter whose fault it is," she said reasonably. "Coupled with tonight, too many rules have been broken. If it's okay with you, I'm asking one of my partners to take over counseling, and I'll act as consultant."

Sensuous, dangerous, mischievous, his dark eyes danced. She wanted to lean closer to see deeper into those coffee brown depths. "That means I can continue to see you without feeling guilty," he murmured.

"I wasn't doing this so we could see each other, Ben." She sounded prim, but couldn't help it. "I'm doing this because the rules were already broken. It's better for Barbie this way."

"I agree," Ben said softly, his mouth tilted in a smile that accented his full bottom lip. "For whatever reason you give."

Sitting back as far as she could, Elizabeth took a deep breath. It was something she didn't seem able to do when she was too close to him. How on earth women resisted his magnetism was beyond her. "Tell me, how long were you married?"

"Okay, we'll do it your way," he said, still smiling. "I was married to Jeanne for nearly a dozen years. She was a wonderful woman with a keen sense of humor. She could tell more about people after talking with them for five minutes than I knew in a year of working with them."

"She was a people person," Elizabeth said, seeing a bit of that quality in Barbie. It needed to bloom, but it was there.

"She never met a stranger. I used to worry about her being so friendly with everyone, but I couldn't convince her to change."

Suddenly his smile slipped and she saw the sadness beneath. "She had so much to give. Jeanne had always wanted a houseful of children, but she was only able to have one. She named Barbie after the dolls she loved and collected. They're put away in sealed boxes right now, but they'll belong to Barbie when she's older. Barbie's not too fond of the name, but she knows where it came from."

"What did your wife do?" Elizabeth asked, using the term "wife" to keep distance between them.

"She was a teacher, but quit when Barbie was born." Ben paused a moment, then went on. She had gone in for a long overdue mammogram, and three days later they called and said something was wrong. I didn't believe them." He gazed down at the ruby red wine, his expression pensive. "Neither did she at first. She fought with everything she had. But later, just before her death, she admitted she'd found the lump in her breast over a year earlier. It had taken her that long to admit she had to do something about it— that's why the mammogram."

"Dear heaven," Elizabeth murmured. It wasn't unusual, but it was so sad. The fear of knowing for certain whether she had cancer had outweighed Jeanne's fear of dying. "I'm sorry," Elizabeth said softly, touching his arm. His shirtsleeve was soft as silk. Who was she kidding? It *was* silk.

He gave a quick smile that disappeared just as fast. "Thanks. I think I've done pretty good adjusting, then I talk about it and realize just how angry I still am."

"And Barbie feels the same way."

His dark brows rose. "Has she said so?"

"Yes."

"I know she misses a woman in her life, but—"

"She misses her mother," Elizabeth corrected.

Ben's dark eyes were filled with such sadness it tore at her. "I can't do a damn thing about it, either."

"Sure you can," Elizabeth said. "Be there for her."

"You're right."

His words warmed her. "It's always nice to hear, Mr. Damati."

"Ben," he corrected softly, pouring a little more wine into her glass. "Now it's your turn. Tell me about yourself."

She watched his strong hands completing the mundane task. Long fingers, a light furring on top of his hands, precision, blunt-cut nails: all combined to show his masculinity—even wearing a frilly apron. It was strange how relaxed she felt being with this man. She was surprised, in fact. He was Mr. Macho in a very sophisticated way.

Reluctantly, she forced herself to pay attention to the question. "There's not much to tell. I was born in Michigan and am the youngest of three sisters. Virginia is a chef specializing in Southwest cuisine in Austin, Texas. Mary Ellen is in Houston and has her own video company. And then there's me."

"Are they married?"

"They both are." Elizabeth had to smile at the thought of either of her independent sisters simpering at some male. "Mary Ellen is just a little superstitious. Last time I spoke to her, she was afraid to talk about it in case the Irish in her changed the pattern of fate."

"She's *that* Irish?"

"*That* Irish," Elizabeth confirmed.

His voice turned coaxing. "And the man in your life?"

His tone reminded her of all the lonely nights and days. She straightened her spine. He wasn't going to seduce her into feeling lonely about not having someone to share them with. "There is none." At his satisfied look, she added, "But you knew that."

He grinned sheepishly. "I knew, but why? You're a beautiful woman."

He was blunt if nothing else. "Because I decided so." She stood and reached for the dirty plates. "I didn't know I needed a reason."

Ben stood, too, and helped clear as if it was the most natural thing in the world. "No, but it's a legitimate question." Once more his body was too close. He bent forward, taking up all her air. "You're talented, intelligent and caring."

She felt her skin warm and her heartbeat race. "Thank you for the compliment."

She placed the dishes next to the sink and confronted him. He stood only inches away and her breath suddenly clogged in her throat. His broad shoulders towering over her shut out everything but the view of him.

His deep, dark brown eyes skimmed her chestnut-colored hair, wide brown eyes, high cheekbones, the tilt of her determined chin. Then rested on her mouth.

Tension seared through her body, sizzled down her spine and rested in places she'd rather not admit to. He was sexy and magnetic, and any woman would be attracted to him. Including her.

"You're right," she said, deciding to answer

his question about the men in her life instead of putting up her usual wall. "I was dating someone, but he couldn't understand why I gave so much time to my career, especially when I don't get paid for half of it. He equated success with money."

Ben's brows rose. "And it's not?"

"No. Success is equated with success. Money is equated with money. Whatever you succeed at is its own reward."

"Of course," he stated dryly. "I should have known."

"You should have." She tilted her head and looked at him, studying his expression. "And I think you do."

"You're right." He smiled. "Shame on them that don't. That guy lost a lot."

She shrugged off the old hurt, dismissing it now. "So it's easier just to do my thing alone."

"What a waste." Ben reached for her waist and slowly pulled her toward him with his strong, capable hands. She felt the hardness of his chest against her open palms. His heartbeat was strong and regular. His smile was sexy and lethal. Words refused to form in her brain. "We're all made to love and be loved, Elizabeth. You're no exception."

"No," she whispered, her mind conjuring up all kinds of images to go with the huskiness of his voice. "Or at least I haven't met the right person to love yet." She cleared her throat and forced herself to stop playing games with images best left alone—such as Ben, naked. "I'm not willing to compromise."

When he replied, his voice was lower still.

"Neither am I. You have too much to give, Elizabeth. It'll take a big man to receive it."

Her chin tilted upward and her eyes flashed. "I'm convinced there's no such animal as my perfect mate."

"Sure there is, you chauvinist." His voice was a mere whisper as he came closer. He bent his head and his warm breath caressed her mouth and throat, making her feel soft and supple and sweet. Sexy. Feminine.

Then his lips slowly, tantalizingly, brushed hers once. *Delicious.* Twice. *Delectable.* Three… She was afraid to move—to breathe—in case he stopped.

He barely touched her, yet her insides heated, melting the ice that had so long enclosed her heart. This was a game to him, something to do to while away the time. He was so very dangerous.…

Yet she wanted more. She wanted to hold him close to her, meld with him, blend their bodies. She wanted to feel the heat of them together as their bare skin touched, wanted to feel the bunched muscles she was sure molded his broad shoulders.…

All thoughts ceased. The scent of spaghetti sauce disappeared. Without realizing what she was doing, Elizabeth rested her hands on either side of Ben's neck, her fingers curled in anticipation of running through the thickness of his dark hair.

When his lips claimed hers, her eyelids drifted shut and she allowed herself to be tucked into the safety of his arms, close to his heart. At his touch, a sudden dizziness afflicted her and she thought vaguely that what she was experiencing must have been like the swoons of yesteryear. She was floating, every one of her senses heightened, with Ben as her anchor.

Lightly she traced the side of his neck. As her fingertips ruffled the hair at his nape, she wondered how he could be at once soft as silk and yet so strong, so solid.

His lips pressed gently against hers, but he didn't make the kiss any more intimate than that. She combed her fingers through his hair again, then slid her hands down to his shoulders.

Yes, she was firmly anchored to his lean, hard body.

4

CANNED LAUGHTER from a TV program made Barbie laugh, and the sound jolted Elizabeth back to the present. As the young girl came closer to the kitchen door, Ben pulled away, dropping his arms. But his dark eyes stared into Elizabeth's, seeing and reflecting the chemistry and confusion she felt. And in his gaze was the promise of another time, another kiss.

As Elizabeth caught Barbie's shadow in the kitchen entrance, common sense flooded back. Her face tinged with embarrassment, she turned quickly, rinsing the dishes they'd left beside the sink.

"Good program?" Ben asked his daughter, his tone light and calm—the opposite of how Elizabeth felt.

"Funny," she confirmed.

Elizabeth glanced over her shoulder. "Pass me some of those dishes, will you?" she asked, keeping her hands busy so she wouldn't throw them back around Ben's neck.

"Better still," Ben said, "why don't you finish up while I continue my conversation with Ms. Gallagher?"

Barbie made a face, but seemed willing. "Okay."

"That's all right," Elizabeth began.

"Come on. I need to finish this discussion." His tone brooked no argument.

She had never followed orders willingly. Ever. But for the life of her, she couldn't find her voice to object.

She didn't want to. She was dying to find out what he had to say—or do. Keeping her hand in his, Ben led her around the corner into the small dining room. She was still slightly breathless and more than a little disoriented from the sensuous promise of his kiss.

Ben looked around the room and seemed satisfied that it was dark and empty except for one battered desk, an outdated computer and an equally battered file cabinet. He spun her into his arms, his smile as compelling as his eyes. Just the look raised her body temperature.

He grinned devilishly. "This discussion will only take a minute. Or two. Or ten," he muttered, seconds before his mouth claimed hers in a kiss that was neither sweet nor friendly. Nor was it chaste. It was electric, sizzling with the promise of red-hot lust. She'd thought the kiss in the kitchen was disorienting, but she'd been wrong. That kiss was nothing compared to this.

This one was fiery and demanding. And it demanded a response from her, as well. She complied instantly, as if a flame had ignited and was suddenly blazing inside her. His mouth and hands warmed her like an expensive, heady brandy. Her muscles weakened; her knees turned buttery. She gripped his shoulders, holding on for dear life.

So this was what he had to say! His actions spoke louder than a thousand words, arousing emotions in her that tumbled on top of each other in mass confusion.

His own breath became short and a low moan echoed deep in his throat, vibrating against her tongue and mouth and sending pinpricks of other sensations through her body.

Several minutes passed before she pulled away. With great reluctance and more control than she had ever had to call on, she finally ended the kiss, resting her quaking hands on his solid chest more for stability than to feel the firm, strong muscles beneath her palms. His heart pounded against her shaking hands and she felt the rhythm echo in her own breast.

After several more moments, she found her voice. "Talk to me, or I'm going back out there with Barbie." It was blackmail, as much for his sake as for hers. She wasn't sure she could avoid temptation and keep herself in line.

Ben's chest heaved with a sigh. "You're one hell of a woman, Elizabeth Gallagher."

"That's quite a compliment, coming from a man wearing an apron."

"See what I mean?" he said with a chuckle. "You're really something."

"Because I can kiss?"

"Because I can kiss you and feel such power," he corrected, but his voice was almost as breathless as hers. "You're one hell of a package."

"All that information in a few minutes. Not bad for a kiss."

"Not bad at all," he said, capturing her mouth once more. "What fun we could have together."

Tension threaded through the sensuality she felt. He wanted to play, and she was taking his game much too seriously. She wasn't the great love of his life, she was just an acquaintance who was willing to play kissie-face in the dark.

That was a sobering thought.

"Talk to me, Ben." This time she meant it.

"Okay, I give." He looked around as if seeing the darkened room for the first time. "Let's sit in the living room for a minute. Okay?"

The living room was devoid of light other than what was coming from the TV, which flickered eerily on the dark walls. Barbie must have pressed the mute button because there was no sound, just the dancing light.

Ben sat on the couch, pulling Elizabeth down next to him. He never let go of her hand. She was glad. She wasn't quite ready to lose the connection.

"I'm sorry if it feels like I'm steamrolling you. I've never been so aggressive before." He gave one of his sexy smiles. "I have to blame the company."

She raised a hand as if to stop him. "Don't blame me. Take responsibility."

He quirked a brow. "For your reaction, too?"

"I'll handle mine. I have my own wet noodle I give myself forty lashes with occasionally."

"I've got a whole collection of them," he admitted wryly. "No one can do guilt better than a single father."

"Try single mothers," Elizabeth stated, glad to

be on less personal, firmer ground. "You have a strong sense of ego and id telling you who you are and what you're capable of accomplishing. And that's good. Despite women's lib, most women haven't yet reached that point of evolution."

He undid the apron and pulled it over his neck. "Yeah, I know." He sounded as if he was quoting by rote as he added, "They have a tougher, rougher, sadder, more rocky road to go than the most Neanderthal of men."

She had the grace to look sheepish. "Sorry. I didn't mean to downplay your problems. I guess I have a different slant." Her free hand rested on his arm, her fingers once more lingering to sooth the silken texture. "I didn't mean...it wasn't my intention to put you, or men in general, down."

"Apology accepted." He smiled once more, dimpling, and Elizabeth felt as if warm sunshine had just entered the room. "What I really wanted to discuss was that I'd be picking you up Sunday around one in the afternoon. Is that all right with you?"

She looked at him blankly. "Picking me up?"

"For the wedding," he said patiently. "Remember?"

In the moment, she'd completely forgotten. "Of course. This Sunday," she repeated. "One o'clock."

"All done," Barbie announced, walking into the living room and plopping herself down on an overstuffed chair. "What are you up to, Daddy?"

He gave Elizabeth's hand a squeeze before letting go, then rested his arm across the back of the couch. "Well, Barbie, I'm trying to make sure Ms. Gallagher is ready when we pick her up this Sunday for your grandmother's wedding." His tone was easy and casual, as if the last quarter hour had held nothing unusual.

Elizabeth wished she felt so at ease. She smiled at Barbie. "Your father invited me to attend the wedding, although I only just found out that your grandmother's the bride. Are you okay with me going?" she asked.

Barbie's eyes lit up. "It's great! That means I won't get stuck at my great-aunt's table while she gossips about how much everyone makes and who's doing what and where!"

"I'm glad you're happy," Ben stated. "It's not every day I get approval from my daughter on my date."

"And I still don't know which grandmother I'm seeing get married," Elizabeth said, her pulse skittering at the word *date*. She supposed it was the correct term, just wished there was another, not quite so intimate one. *Escort* came to mind but that didn't work, either. It sounded more like a service.

"It's my mother," Ben said. "Her name is Linda Lucas and this will be her third marriage. She and my dad split shortly after my fifth birthday. She married two years later, and my stepdad died ten years ago. At that time, she told me she'd already spent the best of her years with the man she loved, and she'd never marry again. Then, five years ago, she met this man—"

"This *wonderful* man," Barbie corrected with a giggle.

"This *wonderful* man," Ben continued, "and has decided to do something she said she'd never do again. In her own words, she's getting married for the very last time."

"How *wonderful*," Elizabeth exclaimed, tongue in cheek. "What's the groom say?"

Both Barbie and Ben laughed. "Not as much as Grandma. But Flynn's a really nice guy. He says he loves her and wants her to be as happy with him as he feels when he's with her. They're writing their own vows and the ceremony will be short and sweet, very different from your traditional wedding."

"And," Barbie said importantly, "Grandma says that they mean the marriage to go on just like the wedding. Different but equal."

"It sounds fascinating." Elizabeth liked the sound of this marriage more than she wanted to admit. There was a bit of the traditionalist in everyone, including her, but there was still room for departure. "I'll be sure to wear something that doesn't embarrass either of you," she teased.

Barbie stopped smiling, her big blue eyes widening as she looked from one adult to the other. "This is what it's like to be part of a family, isn't it?" she asked in a small voice. She blinked several times and tears filled her beautiful blue eyes, shimmering on her long lashes like stars. "That's why I want to keep this baby. It will love me and I'll love it. I'll have a family," she whispered, her voice choked and low.

Ben's voice was harsh in the silence. "Wrong

reason to keep a baby, baby. And don't start crying now."

"I can't help it."

"I can't feel sorry for you when you do that so well all by yourself."

More tears dropped to her cheeks. "That's awful, Daddy."

"No, baby. That's reality." He leaned forward in an attempt to reach her, to make her understand. "What you're defining as family is exactly what I thought we were until you told me differently." He placed his elbows on his knees. "You can't have it both ways, honey. If you and I aren't a family, then you and the baby won't be one, either. Instead, you'll be repeating the exact pattern you say you don't want."

Elizabeth wanted to protect Barbie from the harshness of Ben's words, but he was right. The young girl needed to stop idealizing the baby and the role of being a mama—one of the hardest steps in the process of coming to terms with the situation.

The baby was a miracle unto itself, but not a miracle worker. No child could create world peace, make a family healthier or bond one person to another. Taking care of a small infant was work and hard times, and love and good times. An extension of life.

"You're really mean, Daddy!" Barbie cried, shooting up from her chair. "I hate you!" She bolted from the room, running down the hall to the guest bedroom. It was a surprise when she didn't slam the door shut.

Ben leaned back, his eyes closed as if to erase

the emotionally charged conversation. "I'm sorry to make a scene in your home, Elizabeth."

"I know." She wanted to reach out and hold him until the hurt disappeared, but she knew better. "She needs time, Ben."

"Damn it!" He stood and paced. "Don't you think I know that?" His voice was a low growl that sounded like it was coming from a wounded animal. "But life's not fair and just. It wasn't fair that Jeanne got breast cancer. It wasn't fair that she didn't respond to treatment." He took a deep breath and closed his eyes for a moment. "There are so many survivors out there. Why couldn't she have been one of them?"

"Oh, Ben," Elizabeth whispered. She wished she could help absorb and ease some of his hurt and anger. "I'm so sorry."

"So were we, but it didn't do any good," he said. He buried his clenched hands in his pockets and walked to the window, staring out at the darkness as if there was an answer written on the black velvet sky. "I didn't marry Jeanne for love. Over time, though, I learned to love her."

"I'm glad for both of you."

He ignored Elizabeth's soft comment. "When we first found out about her cancer, I pleaded with the doctor, then God. In the end, I pleaded with the devil." He gave a harsh laugh. "Not even he would listen. It was punishment for marrying a woman I respected and promised to honor and obey."

Elizabeth clasped her hands together, forcing herself not to go to him and stop the flow of words he must have held back for so very long.

She wanted to hold him. Comfort him. Make love to him and ease the pain...

Ben swallowed hard before continuing. "I did everything I could that I thought would make a difference. Then I just did anything at all." He bowed his head, resting his forehead against the cool windowpane. "Anything." His voice dropped even lower. "I took Jeanne to the best doctors, paid for whatever anyone in the medical field ever suggested we try, kept our morale up by spouting lies. Still, I lost her." A single tear ran down his cheek, glimmering in the dull light like a diamond as it clung to his strong jaw. He ignored it. "Ever since Jeanne died, Barbie has acted as if I didn't do enough to save her mother. As if her death was my fault."

He rubbed the back of his neck as if he felt his daughter's eyes on him. "And for years I wondered if I could have done any more or anything different. But I always came up with the same answer. There was nothing else to do." His voice was muffled with emotion. "Jeanne died and I was left with an eleven-year-old girl who missed her mother."

Elizabeth continued to sit quietly on the couch. She finally reached for the cushion to keep herself from reaching out and holding him until the pain went away.

His agony had become hers and tears lit her eyes just as his were falling. He was a good man who didn't deserve this anguish, a man who had gone through so much already and was in such torment. And she didn't know how to ease it.

"I feel as if I'm paying for my sins—only I

don't know which sins they are!" He raised his head and sought an answer in the stars.

"You don't have any," Elizabeth said. "No one does under those circumstances."

She spoke so softly he didn't hear her. "I lost the woman I was supposed to grow old with," he said. "I lost the friendship of my darling baby— the daughter I wanted to protect with my very life. And I lost the world I had worked so hard to create. The world I'd made for all of us disintegrated before my very eyes."

"I'm so sorry."

"It isn't fair." He heaved a deep breath that disguised the sob underneath. "It just isn't fair!"

Elizabeth had stopped thinking as a counselor hours ago. It was heartbreaking to watch a strong and tender man attempt to come to terms with the death of his wife and loss of the family unit. He might not have loved his wife when he married her, but he'd fallen in love with her over the years. That much was apparent.

Elizabeth realized that neither Ben nor Barbie had finished mourning the death of wife and mother, the person who had bonded them together as a family. They had tried a bandage approach to pain, hoping that if they didn't see the wound, it wouldn't be there.

Letting go of the couch cushion, she stood and walked around the edge of the sofa. Coming up behind him as he stood by the window, she wrapped her arms around his waist, holding her palms against his chest. She wanted to give him more comfort than she'd ever wanted anything.

She wanted to wipe away the hurt she knew lay just below the surface.

"I wish I could ease the pain," she said softly. "I wish I could make it disappear for both of you." His breathing was ragged, his heartbeat heavy. The musky male scent that was all his wafted around him and she breathed deeply.

"Hold me," he whispered gruffly, his voice filled with wracking emotions. His hands covered hers and held them to him. "Just hold me."

She rested her cheek against his broad back, feeling the warmth of his skin beneath the smooth texture of his white silk shirt.

In a silence that said so much, they stood for a long time, each receiving solace and comfort from the other.

Things wouldn't change overnight, she knew. She wondered if there was a chance two strong yet vulnerable individuals could heal each other and come to terms with such an intimate death. She prayed to the same God who had turned down Ben's plea for his wife. Maybe this time…

While the night sky sent shooting stars to wish upon, Elizabeth held Ben in the dim light and fervently hoped that those wishes would come true.

ELIZABETH STARED into the full-length mirror.

It had been too long since she'd dressed up and acted like a regular person in a regular world doing regular things.

She was naturally thin, and lately she hadn't eaten as well or as much as she should have, so buying a dress that would accentuate what few curves she had wasn't easy. But she'd been lucky. She'd gone to one of her favorite used-clothing stores and found the perfect dress; it was what used to be called a lawn party gown. Pale green, of lightweight gauze cotton, it was cut with a scoop neck, short sleeves and a tulip-shaped skirt. The waist fit her slim form—well, almost—but the belt made it just a little tighter. The tulip skirt swirled gently around her hips and tummy, flaring into widening gores that flowed around her thighs to fall to just below her knees.

She hadn't seen Ben since three nights ago, when they had all cooked dinner together. Barbie had spent the night again and Elizabeth had driven her to school the next morning. She didn't confront Barbie on her behavior and Barbie didn't say anything that could have opened up the conversation.

The sound of her doorbell stirred Elizabeth into action. When she opened the door, the appreciative look in Ben's dark eyes warmed her through and through. Devouring her with his gaze, eating her bite by tender bite, he smiled slowly as he took in her loose, flowing auburn hair curling around her face, softening her features. He lingered on her neckline, dropping to her slim waist and then down to her toes, only to return to her face. His intimate appraisal made her feel warm and alive and so very feminine.

"Right on time," she said a little breathlessly.

"Couldn't wait," he answered, stepping inside. He closed the door behind him while he continued to stare at her. Although he was wearing a suit, it wasn't the more formal three-piece type she'd seen him in before. This time he wore a cream-colored collarless shirt with no tie anywhere in sight. He looked masculine and wonderful and handsome. "You're beautiful, Elizabeth."

The silver-tongued devil. "Thank you."

"And charming," he said softly. "And delectable." His arms went around her trim waist, pulling her against his body. "And so damn kissable—" He captured her mouth and made her realize just how kissable she was.

Her arms circled his neck, pulling him as close as clothing would allow. His tongue explored her mouth and his hands tightened as he deepened the kiss.

Swooning. *I'm definitely swooning,* she thought hazily. She knew she was right when his hand covered one breast, feeling the size and shape through the light material. She arched into his hand, letting him know just how good it felt to have him touch her. His thumb flicked her budding nipple and she wanted more, so much more....

"Oh, very kissable," he said raggedly, pulling away and reluctantly placing distance between them. "If this wasn't my own mother's wedding..."

She gave a husky, nervous laugh. "I agree."

He grinned, his dark eyes teasing. Or was he? "But I'm sure you could persuade me to be a little late if you chose to."

She shook her head, more to clear it than to disagree. "Think again, Big Boy." With an effort at nonchalance, she grabbed her purse and keys, then headed out the door even though her heart was beating like native drums warning danger. This wasn't a man who was ready for an indepth relationship. "You're the man. You take charge."

He looked disappointed, like a little boy who'd had his favorite toy taken away. "Great, in this day of equality, I still have to act as if I know what I'm doing."

"That's right!" She laughed as she locked the front door and turned toward the car. "Where's Barbie?"

"Still at home. She wasn't satisfied with her dress," he said. "She said it wasn't right, but didn't explain what 'right' was."

"At her age, that could mean anything."

"At any age, it could be anything," Ben corrected, opening the passenger door of his sleek maroon Jaguar. It was as wonderful a vehicle as she'd imagined it would be and Ben drove with an easy hand. They wound around the streets back to his neighborhood, which was in an old and beautiful section of the city. The upright Georgian home on the corner of two wide boulevards looked like an historical antebellum home. Elizabeth's hunch was confirmed when they walked up the steps and she saw the historical plaque next to the door.

"Built in 1862," Ben said, answering her silent query.

"Beautiful."

"Jeanne loved it."

Elizabeth looked at him carefully. "And you?"

Ben shrugged as he unlocked one of the double doors. "It's nice, but I would have preferred something a little more contemporary."

They stepped inside a wide, two-story foyer. An ornate mahogany piano sat directly under the circular staircase. Two short antique pews— the touch of a thousand hands having polished the arms to a dark patina—sat on either side of the door. A rich green Bukhara rug covered some of the sleek, golden oak floor. To the right was a formal parlor, to the left a huge dining area. Both rooms were dressed in period antiques.

Before Elizabeth could comment, a teary wail filled the hall. "Daddy? Is Elizabeth with you?"

"Yes, baby." He took the stairs two at a time. "What's the matter?"

"I can't go," she cried. "Nothing fits. Nothing! I'm big and fat and I can't go to Grandma's wedding!"

Elizabeth followed him up the curved stairs and rounded the corner to an alcove. Barbie sat in the center of the upper hall floor. She wore a short-skirted spandex dress that hugged her barely showing tummy. Although the style was very much in vogue, it did nothing to hide a blossoming figure.

Elizabeth sat down next to Barbie and wrapped her arms around her. "Tough body changes, huh?"

Barbie sobbed and rested her head against Elizabeth's shoulder. "It's so *awful!*"

"Well, I bet if we look together, we'll find something a little more appropriate."

Barbie gazed down at her expensive little creation. "You don't think this is appropriate?"

It wasn't time to lie. "Not now, honey." Elizabeth stood up and held out her hands to the young girl. "I bet we can find something else for this phase of your life."

"I don't have any maternity clothes," Barbie said. "But if I did, I wouldn't want to wear them yet. Not today!"

"You don't have to," Elizabeth said calmly. "All you need to do is find something a little less revealing."

Barbie sniffed, her eyes lighting with hope. "Think so?"

"Think so."

Not letting go of Elizabeth's hand, Barbie stood and led her into a room fit for a princess.... But it was almost too young for Barbie. A large white canopy bed sat along the center of the wall. Pillows in creamy pale satin and deep ruby red were strewn all over. Tiny rosettes and green ferns decorated the wallpaper. Large prints of Victorian children hung everywhere.

Barbie led her to a walk-in closet and stopped. "I don't know what to do," she said. "Everything I have that's dressy is fitted."

"But the wedding isn't really that dressy," Elizabeth said calmly. It was an afternoon wedding so it wasn't formal. It was a third wedding so that usually made it even less so. Ben wasn't wearing a tie....

Elizabeth found a long yellow-and-green gypsy skirt that wasn't body forming. Searching the blouse area, she spotted a yellow T-shirt and tan linen jacket. "Here we go. Let's try this."

Barbie wiped a tear away from her cheek and

made a face. "It doesn't look that good," she said, mistrust in her voice.

"Try it," Elizabeth urged. "And if this doesn't work, come up with something similar. You've got plenty clothes to choose from, honey. Mix and match. Experiment." She gave Barbie a kiss on the forehead. "Your dad and I will be out in the hall, ready to act as fashion police."

She stepped into the large hallway and closed the door behind her. Ben was leaning against the banister, his arms crossed. He looked for all the world like the lord of the manor. But his grateful expression said it all. "Thanks," he said softly. He took her hand in his and led her toward the double French doors at the end of the landing. "We'll be in my study, Barbie," he called, contradicting Elizabeth's last statement.

Once inside the French doors, Elizabeth gazed around, wide-eyed. The furniture was masculine, but still historically correct; the large bedroom was expensively decorated in tones of black, brown and tan, with accents of ruby red. Even the pictures were perfect—just like Ben. "This is your bedroom," she stated.

"Yes." He walked her through another set of French doors on the far side of the room, to what must have once been an open veranda. The clapboard siding was still in place, but the Aubusson rug on top of tan carpeting wasn't part of the original design. He stopped. "And this is my study."

"It's beautiful." She turned full circle. "Your whole house is beautiful."

He sat on the edge of a leather-topped cherry-wood desk. *Real* cherry, she noticed, not a stained imitation. "Thank you," he said simply.

"Your wife had excellent taste."

"Yes, she did." He gave a nod, his voice sounding as distant as his gaze. "But I sold the bedroom furniture we shared and bought what you see. I also bought several of these pieces after she died. The rest of the house, including Barbie's room, is exactly the way Jeanne decorated it."

He gave a sigh. "Someday I'll give the antiques to Barbie for her own home, and I'll buy something a little less...heavy."

Her gaze darted around the room, alighting here and there. "The furnishings in this one room are probably worth what I make in a year. Maybe two."

"Maybe."

She looked around again. The contrast between her home and his was overwhelming. How could he have kept a straight face when he saw her primitive decor?

His gaze narrowed. "Are you going to use money as a wedge so we won't get any more intimate?"

He was frustrating. He wanted intimacy without becoming close. There was no commitment to a relationship, just his desire to take her to bed. What was awful about that was she wanted the same thing, but she also wanted more. And Ben Damati was completely out of her league. The furnishings confirmed it. "There isn't a 'we', Ben."

"I didn't expect a lie." He sounded like a small boy who couldn't get his own way.

"I'm not lying." Her gaze locked with his and she felt the same emotional tug she'd felt the moment they'd met. They might be miles apart socially, but her hormones didn't know it. "Damn." Her lips curved in a small, rueful smile. "I hate getting caught in a lie."

"Come here," he said, opening his arms. His dark eyes warmed and softened, like chocolate syrup, inviting her to partake, to taste, to indulge. "I want to hold you."

With memories of three nights ago, when she'd held him until he'd gained control again, she did as he asked.

Standing between his legs, she melted against his torso. His hands skimmed over the gauzy fabric of her dress, soothing her back and hips as if she were a precious treasure. Wherever he touched her, she burned.

This was what she had yearned for ever since she was a child—someone to care for her, treasure her, love her. She ignored the lusty emotions that flared. For a little while she would suspend harsh reality and pretend this was the culmination of all her childhood hopes.

She rubbed her cheek against his freshly shaved one. His aftershave, a light, musky male scent, was an aphrodisiac, and his firm touch as he held her was addicting. She no longer wanted him—she craved him. Her body warmed at the thought of being held in his arms, in bed, with nothing between them but their own heated breath.

"Daddy?"

Elizabeth pulled away and took a step back. Ben heaved a sigh that told of his regrets, then called over his shoulder, "We're in the study." He remained where he was, his dark eyes still on Elizabeth, speaking volumes as he silently told her things she wanted to hear aloud.

Barbie came to the door, indecision on her face. She looked at both of them and waited for a pronouncement. "Well?"

She was wearing the skirt and jacket that Elizabeth had pulled out of the closet, but she'd found a cotton shell that held all three colors and tied the outfit together. A large French clamp casually held her blond hair at the top of her head. She'd changed into black leather clogs that helped make the outfit contemporary. And she didn't look pregnant.

Elizabeth smiled approvingly. "You look great, Barbie."

The young girl looked relieved, then turned to her father and awaited his judgment. "Daddy?"

"I couldn't have said it better." Ben stood and went to her side, placing a kiss on her forehead. "I'm proud to escort such a beautiful and charming young lady."

Barbie visibly relaxed. "This is the way Daddy likes me to dress, but it's almost too old maidish. 'Cept for a wedding, of course."

"Of course," Elizabeth said with a laugh. "I should have worn an outfit more like that, being an old maid and all."

Barbie looked flustered. "Oh, I didn't mean..."

Elizabeth gave Barbie's slim shoulders a hug

and they all walked toward the stairs. "I'm teasing. Honest."

Once in the car, Barbie became quiet again. She seemed to be dreading the wedding, while enjoying the idea of seeing the relatives.

Ben's mother lived several miles outside of Atlanta, in a beautiful, rambling ranch-style home set back in a two-acre lot. Cars were parked everywhere. Linda looked as if she was barely pushing sixty, though she was a decade older. A small redheaded woman with a mischievous smile that could light up a room, she had a charming, warm and easygoing way about her. But when her gaze was focused on a person, she didn't miss a thing.

"I'm glad Ben brought someone besides my granddaughter," she announced. "Even if you are late."

Ben bent down and gave his mother a quick hug. "I'm not giving you away, Mom. I'm only a guest."

"Of course you're not," she stated firmly in a no-nonsense voice. "A woman doesn't need to be given away in this day and age. I'm neither a parcel of property *nor* a dimwit." She had a twinkle in her eyes, so much like Ben's. "But my son should be present early on this occasion. Besides, Flynn was wondering where you were. He wants to make sure you realize he's making an honest woman out of me after the last five years."

"It's about time," Ben teased. "Your living arrangements aren't a good example for me or my daughter."

"Talk to the federal government. They're the

ones who decided my income would be cut if I made this union legal. I think it's a crime."

"Now, Mom," Ben began.

"Okay, okay, I'll get off my soapbox." She gave his waist a squeeze. "But I'll tell you this, I wouldn't be marrying even now if Flynn didn't feel guilty about living in sin. After all, a commitment is a commitment. What's the point? Am I going to have a baby I need to make legitimate?" The elder woman gave a laugh. "No. I'm just going to lose some social security pension, instead."

Barbie stared hard at the wall. There was a moment of tense silence, but Ben stepped in and smoothed it over beautifully. "You'd marry him anyway. You're just all bluster and no blow," he stated. "You wanted this wedding, too."

His mother grinned widely, her brown eyes twinkling merrily. "Maybe, maybe not. I'm not admitting to anything except that I had a wonderful time putting together this off-the-wall party. That was my payment for going through this fiasco publicly instead of eloping to Las Vegas and having an Elvis impersonator tie the knot. At least that way we could have played the slots."

Although Linda's arm circled her granddaughter's shoulder, her attention was focused on Elizabeth. "What do you do, Elizabeth?"

"I'm a psychologist," she said, not going into detail.

"Not for these two, I hope." Linda glanced at her son for confirmation.

But Elizabeth answered. "No. Not these two."

She could say that with honesty, since she'd spoken to Barbie before dropping off the files on her partner's desk two days ago.

"How did you two meet?"

Ben stepped in. "It's a long story and we'll tell it some other time. What do you want us to do?"

Linda pressed a light kiss on her granddaughter's temple, then dropped her arm. "Greet the guests and make sure everyone knows where the drinks and food are. This is supposed to be casual and fun and just a tiny bit irreverent."

"I'm shocked." Ben sounded anything but.

His mother pointed to the back, where windows marched the full length of the house. Beyond the windows were long tables draped in yellow-and-white cloth and laden with mountains of dainty foods. "There's an open bar on the patio by the pool, and three waiters are walking around with cheap champagne and the best strawberries our local farmers market could drum up. The caterers are taking care of serving, so that's all under control. Herding people through the house is the only problem I have."

"When are you getting dressed, Grandma?" Barbie asked.

The older woman glanced at her watch. "I'd better do it now. I was going to get married in this caftan, but Flynn talked me out of it. He wanted me to wear white."

"White?" Barbie looked shocked. "But Granny, you've been married before. You have children!"

"And I can do what I want, sweets, without censure. I'm old enough to get away with pretending I'm a virgin for the very last time," she stated calmly.

When she earned the laughter she was hoping for, she grinned widely. Her bright gaze wandered around the room, ensuring that everything was the way she wanted it. The doorbell rang and she grinned. "And you can start playing host now, Ben. That's my bunco group, all of whom have daughters they've been dying to foist off on you. Introduce them to Elizabeth and fawn over her a little. That will keep them busy with gossip for weeks."

Linda kissed Ben's cheek, gave it a pat and then disappeared down the hall to what must be the bedroom wing, her bright red caftan wafting behind her like a royal train.

"Welcome to my mother's world—pure chaos," he muttered. But Elizabeth could tell that he was proud to be her son.

A quartet set up on the opposite side of the pool began playing updated classical music interspersed with contemporary jazz.

Barbie gave her dad a kiss on the cheek and promised to check in with him from time to time, then wandered off to find some of her cousins.

"Lucky you," Ben whispered to Elizabeth, his eye on the door as a gaggle of women walked up the steps. "You'll get to meet the relatives after the wedding. They're gathered in their own tight little group waiting to pronounce judgment on you."

"Great." She wasn't going to let their opinion bother her, but the thought of being judged wasn't easy on her nerves. "Just what I wanted—to be found lacking."

"Oh, you won't be," he assured her. "Barbie is the bearer of good news, and that will help. Anything less than thinking you're a gem will not be tolerated."

"You think Barbie will say that?"

"No. I will. Barbie will just growl. Then whine. Then tell them all off if they don't agree with her." His grin was wicked, making Elizabeth laugh. "She doesn't know it yet, but she's got a lot of her grandmother in her."

As several women filed in the front door, Ben held Elizabeth's arm, keeping her by his side. There was a look of panic around his eyes, as if he'd like to bolt at the first opportunity. "Stay with me, Elizabeth, or I'll be fed to the lions," he whispered before greeting the arrivals.

Elizabeth tried hard not to laugh as she covered his hand with hers and gave a squeeze. "You can do this," she whispered during a lull in the excited chatter. Ben still hadn't let go of her arm.

"You know that. My mother knows that. I'm just trying to convince me that *I* know that."

"Poor baby," she whispered, seconds before another small group of women stepped over the threshold and made their way to "little" Benjamin's side for a kiss and introduction. Although he was more than charming to the women who professed to have known him since he was knee high, he obviously had not kept up with them.

Once, Elizabeth leaned over to pick off a piece

of imaginary lint from his shoulder and whispered in his ear, "You're good. Very good."

His grin was positively wicked, his dark brown eyes glinting with sexy innuendo. "I'm much better when I'm alone with you. I'm just waiting for a chance to prove it."

Although she'd started this game, she couldn't think of a single retort, so said nothing.

Half an hour later, Ben showed Elizabeth to one of the lawn chairs, saying "I'll be right back. Flynn just gave me the high sign."

Ben spoke to the band leader, who nodded and smiled. Then, while Ben made his way back to her side, stopping at one table, then at another to pay his respects, the band began playing an old New Orleans jazz number.

To the tune of "Once More, with Rhythm," Flynn strolled out of the patio door from the bedroom wing, casually making his way to the far side of the pool. A huge Magnolia tree spread its branches there, creating a shady haven for the many pots of bright flowers arranged to act as a natural altar.

Flynn was a portly man with a jolly face. He reminded Elizabeth of the perfect relative to play Santa at Christmas. Even his thick shock of gray hair, wire-rimmed glasses and white mustache were perfect for the part. But it was his eyes that drew people to him. He squinted so much from laughter that his eyes could barely be seen; even so, they conveyed his joy with life, which made everyone around him feel good.

The minister, his worn bible clutched in his left hand, watched as the eager bridegroom made his way to the altar. And then Flynn was standing next to the minister, looking expectantly at the sliding glass door. His smile widened and became tender as he watched his beloved Linda walk out of the house and glide over to where he waited. In her hand was a partially opened, salmon-colored canna lily. Against her ecru, waltz-length dress, it looked as vibrant and alive with color as Linda's face.

The bride stopped to squeeze a shoulder of one guest, give a quick hug to another, kiss another's cheek. She even tapped one gentleman on the shoulder with her flower, as if knighting him, which drew laughter. She waved a waiter toward one friend who was out of champagne, then another.

Taking her time to reach Flynn, Linda enjoyed every minute of the process, while her proud-as-punch groom waited patiently for her to complete greeting their circle of friends and join him.

Several members of the family laughed and muttered under their breath that Linda was Linda, and they guessed she wasn't going to change now—thank goodness!

Ben quietly slipped into the seat next to Elizabeth, taking her hand in his as they watched the scene unfold. Elizabeth sensed a little of his tension and she gave him a comforting kiss on the cheek. Each was surprised by her action. "Isn't this wonderful?" she whispered, trying to distract both of them from her spontaneous gesture.

"No. *This* is wonderful," he whispered back. Before she realized what he was talking about, he kissed her partially opened mouth. It wasn't deep or particularly sexy. What it *was* was mesmerizing. Tender. Tears-to-her-eyes sweet. She couldn't look at him for fear of showing him how much that small act meant to her.

Linda and Flynn's vows were short, with Flynn pledging undying love and protection for as long as she would allow him to. The guests might have laughed, except that Flynn had said it with all the love and devotion his gruff voice could muster, and everyone knew he meant the part about loving her until the pacemaker stopped.

But Linda's small speech summed up the ceremony. "Flynn, I pledge my fidelity, my love and my house to you for the next forever. I love you with all my heart, and one of the ways I show it is by bringing you coffee in bed almost every morning. If that's not a commitment from the soul, I don't know what is. I have lived with you and considered us married for the last five years, and the only reason I'm going through with this ceremony is because you've decided that this union needs to be publicly sanctioned in the eyes of the legal system. Our friends already know how we feel, and those who don't don't need to. God already realizes how deep our love is and the commitment we made to each other years ago, so it's no news to Him. I just want you to know that I love you enough to indulge you in this. But don't ask for more."

There was laughter and scattered applause, confirming Linda's sense of humor as well as her love for the big man.

She reached forward and held his cheeks in her hands. "I am so proud to be your life mate, playmate, best friend and lover—just as you are mine. Despite my protest against marriage, you led me toward the life path you stubbornly chose for us. You are such a loving, warm and special man that I realize, against my own words and will, I have fallen in love with the exact right person for me—for the very last time in my life." She cupped his chubby cheeks and kissed him lightly on the mouth. "Thank you, and thank God."

The minister stood straighter, cleared his throat and intoned his small part of the ceremony. But there wasn't a dry eye on the lawn. Linda's heartfelt words touched all the married couples attending, reminding them of their own loving moments.

After congratulations and hugs, the party continued, with more food, more wine and more music. Ben and Elizabeth made their way to the newly married couple, giving their congratulations as well. Flynn couldn't have looked more proud, while Linda just looked relieved that it was over.

Elizabeth was introduced to more relatives and friends. Several of the guests gave Ben the eye, obviously wondering just how intimate their relationship was. Ben's behavior was an enigma to her. He was definitely leaving everyone with the impression that their relationship was serious.

The small band, in deference to the age group, switched to what Ben called, "Big Band sound with an attitude." He pulled her up and into his arms and they moved around the patio to the slow beat. She felt his solid heartbeat against her breast, and her fingers itched to run through his hair. Most of all, her mouth craved his.

"Are you tired yet?" he asked. His face pressed against hers, his mouth less than an inch from her ear. She could stand like this all day long and listen to him whisper. It was a small slice of heaven.

"No, but I can see why you needed me to deflect some of the heat. This is an outspoken group. I gather your family thinks everyone should be married."

"Everyone except my mom and myself. Tried marriage. Been there and done that. Never again."

She ignored the stab in her heart his words caused. "Congratulations on a wise decision. It takes two to make a marriage happy, not one."

"I think so, too." He leaned back, his eyes dancing. "You know what this looks like to my relatives, though, don't you?" he asked.

"No, what?"

"That you're as good as married to me."

Elizabeth's heart skipped a beat. *Keep it light,* she told herself. "There's no such thing as 'as good as'. It's either make an honest woman of me or forget it."

He stared down at her, his expression somber. "Will you repeat that in front of witnesses?"

Her eyes widened. Her heart gave a sharp tug. "No," she said with every bit of calm she could find. "They'll just have to see that actions are the only things that count."

Slowly, he gave a lopsided grin, then kissed the tip of her nose. "You're so bossy, I can't resist," he teased. "Will you go out with me next Friday night? Dinner on the town?"

She couldn't contain the feeling of buoyancy that rocked her. "I'd love to."

His intimate gaze told her just how much he wanted her. Her gaze told him just how compliant she was to his idea. They both silently promised more....

Meanwhile, they danced around the patio, blocking out all others. For just a little while they were alone in their own world.

It was late that evening when Ben and Barbie dropped Elizabeth off at her door. He walked her inside, leaving Barbie in the car with the engine going.

"Thank you," Elizabeth began, turning to face him once she dropped her purse on the couch.

But he touched his lips to hers, waiting for just a fleeting moment to see if she objected. Elizabeth didn't.

The kiss deepened and Ben's arms slipped around her waist, intimately pulling her toward him. She felt the strength of him, the tenderness, and marveled at the way his touch pushed every little button that made her restraint disappear. He tasted her, his tongue slowly, gently taking command of her. She held on to him, feeling his hands drift up her back, then around her shoulders so one hand could cup her breast. The beating of her heart thudded against his palm, she was sure. Her breath zinged through her body, awakening every pore, every nerve.

It was a kiss that promised so much more than what had been before. And when he pulled away, she felt as if she'd lost something precious.

"I'll see you next Friday," he murmured.

She found enough breath to say one word: "Yes."

"This relationship will go further. You know that." His voice was low and husky, but very sure.

She was a psychologist. There was no sense in prevaricating. Her thoughts were consumed with him. Her heart was already involved. "I know," she whispered.

He kissed her one more time before reluctantly leaving.

Once the taillights disappeared, Elizabeth wished she hadn't been so forthright. All she had to do was be honest with herself.

Just thinking about his kiss made her heart quicken, her hands become damp. Her stomach clenched.

Next time they met, she'd be more circum-spect. She'd be damned if she'd wear her heart on her sleeve.

Laughter sounded in her head. That plan hadn't worked today. It probably wouldn't work tomorrow.

5

TAPPING A PEN against his leather-bound desk blotter, Ben stared idly out his study window. His thoughts were ten miles away, in a small house on a tree-lined street where a fascinating woman lived. They were stream-of-consciousness thoughts that skipped like rocks on water.

From the first moment he saw Elizabeth Jean Gallagher, he'd been physically attracted. He'd been a widower for nearly six years and he'd never felt that strong a pull to any woman—before or after Jeanne. And certainly not with a woman like Elizabeth. She was independent, a women's libber, psychoanalyzing and quick tongued. But she was also sexy as hell, and that called to him like a beacon lighting up a harbor in the night.

Elizabeth wasn't like most women he knew, including his late wife; she was just the opposite. Elizabeth even enjoyed his mother, her off-beat sense of humor and quirky nature.

He grinned. In many ways Elizabeth reminded him of his mother. Both women were ready to fight the good fight, right wrongs by speaking out, help people find their paths, give lectures on good and bad. In general, they were both opinionated.

His mother was a special woman. Willful and just a little wacky, she'd raised him to be a man of principle. Of morals. Of traditions.

He had hoped he'd done the same thing with his daughter. And to prove it, he wanted Barbie at least to ask to marry the boy who'd helped create her child. He certainly wouldn't allow it, but he wanted Barbie to want that. A man who met his obligations was a man people could trust. Ben ought to know. He'd met one of those trust issues head-on early in his life.

He hadn't told Elizabeth about the roots of his marriage yet. It wasn't important, he'd told himself, but he wasn't sure that was true. He wasn't sure he wanted to break open that egg....

His daughter was a puzzle to him, one he couldn't understand. She was suddenly a loose cannon, a girl he didn't know how to raise and whose sexual secrets he didn't know how to deal with.

He hadn't known where to turn when he'd found out his precious baby was pregnant, so he'd blamed himself. Where had he failed her? What had he done wrong? Why hadn't he seen it coming? He'd had a thousand questions, no answers.

Then his secretary had recommended Elizabeth. Ben had been drawn to her the first moment he'd seen her.

Elizabeth's actions attested to the fact that she liked the physical side of their relationship— what little physical side there was. But if he couldn't get past her duck-and-dodge attitude, he'd never get her into his bed.

Physically, he was stunned by his reaction to her. He wanted her in his arms in the worst way. She ignited the sexual side of him as much as she did his intellectual side. He just hoped he could convince her she felt the same about him. It wouldn't be easy, but he was confident he could do it. Making tough sales was part of what he did for a living, and he'd been very successful in a difficult field.

As an architect who specialized in designing prisons, Ben was fascinated with enclosures. What were the best ways to detain people while still giving them the necessities of life: work areas that were bright and spacious; courtyards with both sun and shade; play areas for lifting weights or jogging, vital outlets of energy, that also allowed guards to see every inch of the grounds? Security was another big issue—safety for guards, workers and inmates alike. Ben had to be up on the latest in electronic equipment.

He'd worked hard setting up his own company, harder still at gaining contracts based on his visions. But it worked. Now he had his own architectural firm that employed five other architects and dozens of draftsmen and computer technicians. They worked full time designing facilities across the country as well as in Europe and Canada.

Until the year before Jeanne's death, he'd devoted all his energies toward his business, while she had devoted her life to their child and home. Each had found an all-consuming career, almost excluding the other because there was no time left for both.

Oh, Jeanne had loved him. And although he'd never really felt that elusive emotion, he had cared for her in his own way and had called whatever it was he'd felt love. There was no doubt he cared for her, but there were no drums beating, no quickened breath, not even anticipation at being with her. In fact, most of their married life had been downright staid. He knew it had to do with his feelings, but he hadn't known how to change the situation.

Jeanne and he had drifted steadily apart, each becoming autonomous out of necessity. She'd told him of the household events; he'd informed her of upcoming business trips. She'd let him know about balanced bank statements, clothing that was picked up from the cleaners or bought and put in the closet. Together, they'd juggled social engagements.

And of course, they'd discussed their daughter and her latest escapades, cute sayings, problems. Those conversations took place in brief moments they managed to find together one or two evenings a week. The rest of the time they spent in their own worlds, doing their own things.

He'd lived alone in the house with his family.

God, he hated admitting that! But deep inside, he'd known it and hadn't bothered to change the pattern. He'd grown accustomed to being alone. It was the best of both worlds. He could talk about his wife and daughter, and yet he could live his own life.

Jeanne's cancer had changed their family routine. This time, instead of focusing on their independent lives, they'd focused on doing everything necessary to eliminate the killer in their midst, while still preparing for the inevitable. They'd been together at last, yet not really.

Jeanne had once said that the rush to find a "fix" was like letting her feet make decisions while the right foot was in the grave and the left foot was on a banana peel. She was right. They'd never made a decision that wasn't based on her illness or that didn't serve as a bandage to her problems. They'd become unified against a disease, secretly knowing all the while that they were fighting a losing battle.

And in the end, the battle *was* lost. Ben was left with a child he and Jeanne had forgotten to include in their private conversations, in the agonizing decisions that continued until her death. They'd thought they were protecting Barbie, their sweet doll, their perfect child.

Instead, they had isolated her from their lives.

Ben heaved a tired sigh. He was trying to bring Barbie back into his life or gain entrance into hers. But he was failing. He didn't know how to do it, and she shut him out at every turn. Just as he had done to her for so very many years.

His big mistake was thinking that he and Barbie could get along like he and Jeanne had, mixing in each other's worlds for a while, then going off to live separate lives. He'd forgotten Barbie had issues, too. He'd taken her loss for granted, so that when her anger flared, he wasn't prepared for it. Feeling sorry for himself, he'd forgotten her heartache, her needs.

He'd also forgotten how to hope.

Then Elizabeth came along. She was the perfect diversion, as well as a reminder of better times. Intelligent and pretty, she could also help him relate to Barbie. It was a great combination. Elizabeth gave him back his hope.

"Damn."

Until meeting her, he wasn't sure he had wanted that particular feeling again. But she'd awakened hope in him whether he liked it or not.

Ben smiled, thinking about Elizabeth. She was scared, but she couldn't disguise the fact that she was interested in him on a physical level. She showed him with every sultry look and smile, and the delightful way her eyes lit up when he came into the room.

Ben doubted he would ever know the kind of love that songs were written about and poets waxed lyrical over. He doubted it existed, but he could still be drawn into a woman's web. That was apparent by his reaction to Elizabeth.

He gave a stretch, a feral smile playing around his lips. It was time for action. He picked up the phone and dialed Elizabeth's home number, leaving a message at the sound of the beep.

Once more, hope welled up inside him.

WHEN ELIZABETH WALKED OUT to the parking lot at lunchtime, Ben was leaning against the fender of her car. He looked better than a sunny day and sexier than any movie star hunk she'd ever seen. His dark eyes twinkled as he studied her walking toward him, and openly appreciated her from top to bottom. "The beautiful Ms. Gallagher, I presume."

"What are you doing here?" she asked, shocked into forgetting her manners for the moment.

"I brought a picnic lunch and thought you might enjoy helping me eat it."

Regret shot through her. So did excitement. "I'm so sorry. I just don't have time for a long lunch right now," she said, glancing at her watch. "But I'll take a rain check."

Ben smiled confidently. "How much time do you have?"

She did a quick mental calculation. "At the most, forty-five minutes."

"Good enough." Satisfaction laced his voice. He pushed away from her car and opened the door of the Jaguar, parked next to it. "Get in. We're wasting time."

"Where are we going?" she asked, while she did as he ordered.

"The little park down the street," he answered, shutting her door. "It's just a few blocks." He slipped into the driver's seat and started the car.

"I don't know," she said, still hesitant, still a little afraid. She was beginning to get too involved with this man. She had a feeling he wasn't the kind who would allow anyone to get too close.

"I'll have you back in the same time it would have taken for you to eat at some fast-food joint." He raised his hand, the gold band of his expensive watch glinting in the sunlight. "Promise."

Her mind whirred with possible reasons for

this impromptu lunch. "Nothing has happened to Barbie, has it?"

Ben put the car in gear and backed out. "Nope."

"Are you all right?"

Ben slipped into traffic and stepped on the gas. "Right as rain," he answered.

"Is there a problem I don't know about?" she persisted. "Your mother is all right, isn't she?"

"She's on her honeymoon, shell hunting with Flynn on some white, sandy Mexican beach. I'd say she's fine."

Elizabeth tilted her head and studied him, puzzled. "Then what's the matter?"

Ben pulled off the road and drove down to the bend in the river. "Nothing."

Something had to be wrong. Otherwise, why would he bother coming this far from his own office in the middle of the day? They weren't dating or involved. Not yet. Not ever, she reminded herself.

"Then why all this?" She waved toward the picnic basket in the back seat.

Ben parked the car under a tree and rolled down the windows so they could hear the stream rushing over rocks just feet away. He turned in his seat to face her. "I brought lunch because we both have to eat and I thought it would be nice to have some peace from the outside world. Just the two of us. We—" he pointed first at her, then at himself "—as in you and me."

Her mouth formed a perfect O, her eyes widening as she watched him lean closer.

"So relax," he said, his voice dropping down an octave, turning low and rough. "Enjoy."

He smiled one of those slow, easy smiles that eeked of confidence. He leaned even closer.

Elizabeth's breath caught in her throat; her gaze locked on his lips. She sat completely still for a moment, her mouth becoming dry, dusty. Her heartbeat quickened, pulsing in her throat like a drum. Without realizing it, she leaned toward him. Toward his mouth…

Ben reached in the back seat and brought the picnic basket forward. "Would you like red or white wine?"

Her breath whooshed from her lungs. A pink flush tinged her cheeks as she realized just how much she had craved the kiss she'd been expecting.

Swallowing her disappointment, she sat up a little straighter and watched as he opened the basket and reached inside. "Neither," she said primly. "I have an appointment in a little while."

He grinned and her heart melted a little. "I thought you'd say that, so I brought iced tea." He handed her a glass container. "And low-fat sandwiches."

"How did…?"

He shrugged, as if it was an everyday thing, but his eyes grazed her slim figure. "I guessed."

Windows open, light breeze blowing, they snacked quietly. Elizabeth kept her eyes on the joggers passing by. Birds swooped down, occasionally dive-bombing some of the slower walkers who got too close to their nests.

Ben guessed her thoughts. "Must be babies nearby."

She smiled, relaxing for the first time in several days. "Must be," she murmured, stretching her legs.

Ben took another bite, then tossed the crust of his sandwich in the basket. He leaned forward, very close to her now. "Have dinner with me tonight."

"I can't." It was an automatic response.

He leaned toward her until they touched. This time there was no misunderstanding his intentions. He wanted a kiss. He wanted *her* kiss. All the tumbling, topsy-turvy emotions he'd raised the night they'd cooked together at her house came slamming through her again. She wanted him to kiss her. She hated feeling so driven by lust.

He brushed his lips against her parted mouth. A need began building, warming, heating, filling her with wonder. "Please," he murmured.

She wanted another kiss. No, she didn't. Yes, she did. Elizabeth didn't know what she wanted, so she stuck by her guns. She forced herself to speak with his lips just millimeters away from hers, his warm breath teasing her mouth. "Not until Friday. We agreed."

"Dear lady," he sighed, rueful exasperation lacing his words. He pulled away from her and leaned back in his seat. "You could make a saint sin."

She took a deep breath and moistened her lips with a dainty lick of her tongue. Then, pretending that nothing unusual had happened and that she hadn't reacted, she casually tossed the remainder of her own sandwich into the basket. She didn't want to admit how absurdly bereft she felt that he wasn't being more persistent. "I'm sorry." He looked so comically sad and frustrated, Elizabeth laughed. "You're nuts."

He was darling, even with that smug expression, which should have set off warning bells on its own. A man didn't get this cute without having had lots of practice on other women. "It's just one of the many reasons you love me," he stated.

"Sure." She grabbed a brush from her purse and ran it through her hair. Small habits kept her focused on the ordinary instead of on Ben. Sexy, wonderful, masculine Ben. Lethal Ben. "But just the same, would you take me back to the office?"

"In a minute. I promise I won't let you be late," he said. "But right now, take a moment to stare through the sunroof at the canopy of trees and listen to the rushing water. And relax."

He leaned his head against the headrest and did what he'd just suggested she do. Then he reached over and clasped her hand, erotically stroking it with his thumb.

After ten minutes enjoying the blessed silence, the soft breezes, he gave a long, satisfied sigh. "Nice."

"Yes," she said, not moving. She was far more relaxed than she had been, but she couldn't relax completely—not with Ben sitting next to her, touching her.

He slowly turned his head and looked at her. Just as slowly, he leaned over, his mouth just inches from hers. She waited, wanting desperately to flee or wrap her arms around him, she couldn't tell which. His smile was disarming. "Do I have to beg for a kiss?"

Her heart tugged with want. "If you insist," she said, her voice barely above a whisper.

"Oh, yes," he said, his voice equally soft and sounding twice as determined. "I insist. It's the least you can do, since you broke my heart."

"Baloney." It was a whisper.

His mouth ate the word, covering hers with a tender firmness that set her heart on fire. One hand cupped her neck, holding her in the palm of his hand. His lightly callused thumb traveled down her neck, feeling the pulse at the base. Heating her. His kiss started out tender then became a branding iron—hot and searing. She didn't know when she brought her hand up to his face. She didn't know when she started running her fingers through the springiness of his thick, dark hair. It didn't matter. She wanted more—so much more. Her body reacted to Ben as if he were a powerful drug and she was addicted.

When he pulled away, she gave a small moan, an unexpected sound that echoed hollowly in the car. She didn't want the kiss to end. She didn't want to leave the sensuous haven of his arms.

Ben smiled, reminding her of a tiger, looking tame and sleek but ready for the kill at a moment's notice. The fleeting look in his eyes matched the way she felt inside.

"Thank you." His voice was quiet, his expression suddenly calm as he moved away. With a flick of the wrist, he started the car and drove her back to the office.

She told herself to relax. She could be just as cool. She could maintain her presence of mind.... Ben pulled up in front of the office and she gave him a brittle smile. "Thanks for the break."

"You're welcome." Just as she was about to step out of the car, he gave her a chaste kiss on her cheek. No pressure. No promises. "One more thing," he said, reaching into the back. From the floorboard, he picked up a small white box with a gold bow on top. "This is just a reminder of what you planted inside my head."

"Ben, I can't," she began, her eyes big and wide and just a little worried.

"It's nothing. Honest. Just put it on your desk and enjoy it. I bought it instead of flowers."

Elizabeth weighed the package in her hand for a second. Then a smile burst through. There was nothing wrong with accepting flowers; there'd be nothing wrong with accepting the equivalent. "Thank you."

"You're welcome. See you Friday night."

With a quick smile and a wave, she was back in her office, feeling as if she'd been gone a week instead of a lunch hour. And she wanted him to come back and kiss her again. Stroke her. Make her laugh. Now. Her nerves sang. Looking back at the time they'd just spent together, Elizabeth realized his goal had been to make her aware of him as a sexy, sensuous man—just in case she hadn't noticed. She had to give him credit. He'd done what he set out to do; she was aware of him in every fiber of her body.

She felt brilliantly alive. Until he'd touched her, a part of her had been asleep. He had awakened her out of a quiet life of nothingness and made her aware of her femininity once more. She hadn't wanted him to know that's what he had done. But now he did.

She waited until Darlene, the receptionist, left before opening the small box. Inside, wrapped in white tissue paper, was a small ceramic jar sealed with a cork. The painting on the little jar was what made it special. Small bunches of violets circled the creamy white vase, and on two sides the word *Hopes* was written in italics. She worked the jar and looked inside. There was a folded piece of paper there. She lifted it out. In neat handwriting, it said: "I hope I can wait until Friday night before I see Elizabeth again."

Her laughter bubbled up. The man was a whiz at getting behind her defenses. He had all the right moves.

She placed the small ceramic jug in the middle of her desk so her clients could see it, too.

Throughout the next session, the memory of Ben holding her hand while she leaned back and stared at the sky kept popping into her head. Recalling every expression that had crossed his face, she relived the moment when his head had come down to claim her mouth. It was a wonderful, exciting, just-for-the-fun-of-it-and-because-you're-fantastic kiss that had curled her toes and made her never want to stop. Although she knew he wasn't serious about making this relationship anything more than fun and sex, she suddenly didn't care. For the time being, it was worth it to be with him.

Why not enjoy each other's company?

JUST BEFORE CLOSING the clinic, Elizabeth sat on the edge of her partner's desk, her forehead creased in a frown. She had been listening to the details of Marina's last session with Barbie. The young woman was still full of tension and fear, but she was dealing with her problems a little better than she had been at first.

Marina sat back and closed the file in front of her. "Well, Barbie's decided to carry the baby full term while going to the classes for pregnant girls in her school district. I've asked her to wait until she's further along before she decides whether or not to give up the baby for adoption. I explained that either decision was a good one and assured her that there is nothing dishonorable about allowing someone without children to love and raise your baby."

"She's still undecided, though, isn't she?"

"Yes," Marina said, her dark head bobbing. "But, like I said, this isn't a decision that has to be made today."

"Good advice." Elizabeth thought for a moment. "Did she mention her father?"

"Of course." Marina glanced down at the open file in front of her. "Her perception of him seems to be a little more realistic since the first time I spoke to her. But then she's not as panicked. As she gets further into the pregnancy she's beginning to realize that the world didn't really come crashing down around her head the way she first thought it would."

"And she's not quite as defensive," Elizabeth guessed.

Marina smiled. "Not quite. But she still doesn't want to talk about the father of this baby. I'm pretty sure she has dreams of that young twerp coming to 'rescue' her from all this and riding off into the sunset."

"You think so?"

Marina's rolled eyes and raised eyebrow told the story. "The girl still believes in fairy tales. Maybe even more so because her mother wasn't there to guide her through the relationship jungle of adolescence."

"And her grandmother has lived her own life and isn't really close enough to be easily accessible. No women friends in sight."

Except Marina, now her therapist, and Elizabeth, who was—what? Barbie's used-to-be therapist? Her father's wannabe lover? "This is so hard," she said, more to herself than Marina.

But her partner knew what she was saying. "Isn't it just as simple as can be? Ben wants you. You obviously want him or you wouldn't have handed Barbie to me. Go for it."

Elizabeth was surprised. "An intimate relationship with Barbie's dad?"

Marina nodded. "Any man who thinks it was a mistake to name his daughter after a doll can't be all bad," she stated with conviction. "Besides, it's obvious he's as interested in you as you are in him. It's about time for both of you. So go have a fling. Enjoy."

Elizabeth gave a wry grin. "Thanks for your blessing, but it's not that easy."

"Why not?"

"Because..." Elizabeth faltered, wondering what reasons she could give that would appease Marina. She remembered the kiss this afternoon and felt a warm blush in her cheeks.

Marina saw the tinge of pink. "Because you're scared and you've vowed never to get involved?"

"How'd you know?"

"I'm your partner, remember?"

"Okay. But this guy is dangerous to my libido."

"No, *you're* the dangerous one. To yourself," Marina added.

"What in heaven's name are you talking about?" Elizabeth exclaimed, irritated by the way the tables had suddenly turned.

"You seem to think you don't deserve happiness with a man in your life, either that or you think there *is* no happiness, with *any* man."

"That's not true."

Marina gave her a pointed look—the kind that said, "Yeah, right, and you never lie to your tax man, either."

Elizabeth stood and smoothed her skirt, readying to leave. "Okay, Ms. Philosopher," she said in her most distant voice. "I'll think about it."

"Great. Just remember, I'm here for you."

"Ditto," Elizabeth muttered. "Whatever that means."

Marina wasn't willing to let it go. "It means that although we might not be talking to each other tomorrow, you can call if you need me, and I'll be right by your side.''

The anger left Elizabeth's body. She was still irritated, having heard something she didn't want to face, but her frustration had nothing to do with Marina. "Thanks, partner. See you later.''

As she walked down the hallway, she discarded Marina's words, unwilling to look any closer at what might be the truth. Perhaps another time...

But when she sat at her desk and phoned the answering machine at home, she realized that Marina's observations might bear studying. She stared at the little "Hopes" jar as she listened to her messages.

Ben's rough voice was low and sexy and the sound rasped against her insides, igniting a warm glow. "Hi, Ms. Elizabeth Jean Gallagher. This is Mr. Benjamin Damati, and I'm asking for a date sooner than Friday. May I take you to the movies tomorrow night? There's a wonderful comedy at the mall theater, and since it's Thursday there shouldn't be as big a crowd as there would be on the weekend. I'll call you this evening for your answer. If you say yes, I promise I'll buy you the biggest box of popcorn they have, along with all the chocolate-covered peanuts you can eat. How's that for a bribe?''

There was a smile in his voice, and Elizabeth felt an answering one deep in the pit of her belly.

Nevertheless, her first response was to say no, which made her wonder.... Was Marina right? Was she afraid? Was any man a threat to her?

Yes. The answer rang clearly in her thoughts before she could censor them. But why?

Before Elizabeth even realized what she was doing, she picked up the phone and dialed her oldest sister. It was late afternoon, so Virginia would be at the office—a catering kitchen in her husband's computer-fabrication building. According to Virginia, the company nursery was right next door, which still wasn't good enough. Virginia kept the baby in the kitchen-tasting area until nap time, then allowed her to sleep next door. For Virginia, it was the perfect world.

Elizabeth relaxed when she heard her sister's voice on the other end of the phone. "Well, I just thought I'd touch base with you. Did I interrupt any great new recipes?" she asked.

"It's about time a member of my family called to see if I had eaten myself into oblivion in this business. For all you know, I could weigh three hundred pounds by now."

Hearing Virginia's good-natured complaints brought back a flood of fond memories. The image of her tinier-than-a-minute sister being overweight was funny. Elizabeth laughed, but Virginia wasn't fooled. "So, darlin' what's the problem that you would call your oldest sister about?"

"Who said there has to be a problem?"

Virginia scoffed. "You did! Remember a few years back you told me that no one calls out of the blue without wanting something?"

"Lord, I'm getting way too open with my family if they can toss my own words back in my face," Elizabeth stated dryly, but they both knew she was kidding.

"That's what you get," Virginia said, popping what was probably some flavorful morsel into her mouth and speaking around it. "When are you coming to visit your dear sweet big sister who's several inches shorter in stature but not in advice?"

"Soon," Elizabeth promised, wishing they were together right now. "Very soon. But first, I want to ask you something highly personal. This therapist needs a little focus."

"Hold on and let me go somewhere a little more private," Virginia volunteered. Then, after a few moments of silence, she came back on line, her tone serious. "What's up?"

Her sister's willingness to listen brought tears to Elizabeth's eyes. Family was so important— even when they weren't right next door. "Have you ever known me to be afraid of men?"

"Not afraid of men, no."

"Afraid of what, then?" Elizabeth prompted.

Virginia's answer was quick and to the point. She didn't even have to think about it. "Afraid of a relationship," she said. "Ever since Daddy died, you've acted like men would automatically walk out on you if you started up a relationship. Since his death, you've kept your distance with every guy I can remember. Sometimes I think you deliberately chose some guys because you knew they'd be unreachable or totally shallow. Some people would say it's a need to be in control. I call it fear of abandonment."

"Abandonment?" Elizabeth repeated dumbly,

the word not registering. "You're saying this has something to do with Daddy dying?"

Anyone else would have hemmed and hawed. Not Virginia. Right or wrong, she'd state her opinion. "Yep. That's exactly what I'm saying. It's as if you're afraid to make a commitment because if you do, he'll leave. Just like Daddy did."

"That's silly. Daddy couldn't help dying."

"Exactly. But while Mary has always been the timid one of us three sisters, you, my dear, have always been the scared one, even though you seldom show it. Don't ask me for any more analysis. That's your department."

"I still say that's illogical."

"Why? Where Daddy was concerned, you were always a pushover. You were the youngest, so you saw him as none of us did—as a wiser, more gentle man. He was in a different stage of his life when you were little. For the last in the nest, it sometimes happens that way."

"You're saying that I have issues to work out about Daddy," Elizabeth said.

"No," Virginia replied. "I'm saying you have a hang-up about Daddy leaving you, and that spills into your love life, which, if I'm not mistaken, is still nil. *You're* calling it an issue."

Elizabeth groaned. "I hate it when you're a know-it-all!"

Virginia laughed. "I know. It's hard to take, isn't it?"

"From now on, I'm calling Mary Ellen."

"Good luck. I can't reach her most of the time. She's so busy with the architect, redoing the house she bought and turning it into the studio of her dreams. She's even building a garage apartment for her secretary and friend to live in as caretaker. Edie's her name, I think. Turns out the woman is going through a tough divorce and starting again."

Elizabeth wasn't going to mention that Ben was an architect. In fact, she wasn't going to mention Ben, period.

"Well, now that we've solved the problems of the world—"

"Of the Gallagher family," Elizabeth corrected.

"The Gallagher family *is* the world as far as I'm concerned. It's *our* world."

"I'll remember that," Elizabeth promised dryly. "Well, thanks, sis. I'm heading home to my hot dog with chili sauce and my thirteen-inch TV, and I'm going to pretend we didn't have this conversation." Fat chance. Virginia, the down-to-earth philosopher, had opened up too many possibilities for her *not* to think about things.

"Wait!" her sister demanded. "You can't go without telling me about the guy."

Elizabeth wavered. Then, giving in to the inevitable, she told her about Ben. What was the use of pretending he wasn't in her life? If she lied, it would suggest that Ben was important to her. Her sister knew her too well for that. Besides, Elizabeth had called to get an opinion, and she might as well go all the way and get one.

When she was finished, Virginia whistled into the phone. "You know what I would do if I were you?"

"What?" Elizabeth asked dryly. "Run?"

"Go for it," Virginia said calmly, ignoring Elizabeth's suggestion. "If it doesn't work out, you haven't lost anything that you had before. If it does—well, there's no end to the wonderful things that come with real relationships."

"He doesn't seem to want a 'real' relationship. He's a widower. I think he's just looking for a little fun."

"What makes you say so?"

"Because he's never hinted at commitment or relationship, in either past or present tense. Come to think of it, he hasn't even admitted to loving his wife."

"Go for it, anyway. You can always change his mind."

"Who's the therapist here?" Elizabeth asked with a laugh.

"Who called who?" Virginia countered, a smile in her voice. "Listen, I've got to run. It's Ruth Anne's feeding time and I'm the bottle. My sweet is daintily screaming at the top of her well-formed lungs. But I'll call soon. I want the next installment of this story."

"It's not a story yet. Not the way you mean it, anyway."

"Well, fish or cut bait, darlin'. Now's the time. Wonderful men aren't standing on every street corner, you know."

"Who says every woman needs a man?" Elizabeth knew she sounded defensive, but she couldn't help it. There was only so much she was going to learn in one lesson—especially from her sister.

"No one. But you want this one. You're just

afraid to reach out and grab happiness with both hands. What is it Wilder used to say? Oh, yes. 'Go for the gusto!' I repeat his sentiments.''

"Well, now that we've got everyone in on this, I'll say goodbye.''

She heard a blood-curdling scream in the background. Her new niece. "Before you defend your 'no' answer, goodbye, little sister, and I'll talk to you soon," Virginia said quickly. "I love you.'' The line clicked, then went dead.

Still smiling, Elizabeth switched to a new line and called Ben's answering machine. "I'd be happy to go to the movies Thursday on the conditions you stated. Except that I also want toffee or the deal's off. See you then.''

After completing the paperwork for the day, Elizabeth sat in deep introspection. She was a darn good therapist, but she hadn't seen her own shortcoming. Her sister had diagnosed her problem right away, which meant Elizabeth had been living in a fairyland. She thought she'd hidden her inadequacies from her siblings. "Amazing,'' she muttered. "Damn.''

Disturbing as the thought was, though, it was comforting to know that someone out there knew her with all her faults, and loved her in spite of them.

BEN CALLED THREE TIMES during the day. She relished each and every call. He told her jokes that made her laugh and reminded her of their picnic, which made her feel good about herself. And then he reminded her of his attraction to her, which made her feel sexy and wanted.

By the time she parked in her driveway, she was a bundle of nerves.

She jumped when the doorbell peeled an hour later. Staring through the peephole, she saw Ben on the other side of the door, looking back at her as if he could see right through the wood. He looked just as sexy as ever in his usual uniform: expensive suit pants, matching vest and a striped shirt. His tie was missing and the top button of his shirt was undone to expose the tanned column of his throat.

She opened the door and looked through the screen. He didn't say a word, just stared back, enveloping her with his dark eyes.

Slowly, she smiled.

So did Ben.

She pushed the screen door open and he stepped through, wrapping his arms around her before the door was closed. He stared down at her slightly parted mouth, and her breath caught when she saw the promise in his gaze. Very slowly, as if drawn by a magnet, his mouth brushed hers. Then brushed again. He tightened his arms around her slim waist, pulling her closer to the hard, masculine contours of his body.

"What a nice hello," he finally said, pulling away enough to press his cheek to hers. "We ought to meet like this more often."

"We're not going to the movies tonight," Elizabeth stated, resignation and desire in her voice. His intention had been written all over his face before she'd opened the door. She ought to know. She felt the same way. "We're going to make love tonight, aren't we?"

"Yes." He was positive. No doubts. No fears. Just an honest answer.

Relief flooded her, easing the restless tension in her body and turning it in another direction—to the pit of her stomach where it settled as an ache. "At last."

"At last," he repeated. His hands wandered up from her waist to cup her small breasts in his palms.

She held the sides of his face, loving the feel of his strong jawline beneath her palms. She looked into his dark eyes and saw the kindness. The need. It matched her own.

"Kiss me," she murmured.

His groan told her just how much need he was leashing. She loved the feel of his mouth on hers. His warm breath on her cheek. They kissed until she was heady with delight. Dizzy with it. And when he pulled away, she didn't want it to end. His hand cupped her head, holding it to his broad chest as if he was afraid of losing her. She smelled his freshly laundered shirt, the fabric softener, his aftershave. All the scents merged into his own, very special mixture.

"Where?" he asked, his voice so rough with need.

"My room," Elizabeth said, pulling away. With more confidence than she felt, she took his hand and led him down the hall.

When they got to the side of the bed, Ben turned her around. "My treat. I get to undress you," he said softly.

"You don't have to," she said, thankful that the room was shadowy. She wasn't voluptuous or curvy or sexy looking. She was too thin....

"I want to," he said, making that sound like a harsh demand. "I've dreamed of doing this. Don't deprive me now."

He reached for her, and the sound of her skirt zipper being pulled down might have been a siren in the still evening air. The only noise louder was Elizabeth's light, shallow breathing. Her skirt fell to her ankles in a puddle. Her black panties were starkly contrasted with white skin.

Ben's breath rasped harshly in the silence as he pulled the fabric of her blouse away from her skin, then slipped one button through its hole. And then another, exposing more and more soft skin. By the time all the buttons were open, Ben's eyes were glinting with desire. He slipped his warm hands inside and slid them up over her rib cage to stroke her shoulders before lightly pushing the shirt off her arms. It fell to the floor, joining her skirt.

Elizabeth stood in her black panties and bra, breathlessly watching the myriad expressions crossing Ben's face. "You're so beautiful," he said quietly, at last. "You have no idea how beautiful you are."

"I'm too skinny," she offered, afraid to believe him. Afraid to be all that he wanted.

"You're perfect." His gaze came up to meet hers and she saw the need and awe in his eyes. "But you could be the size of an elephant and still be perfect."

It was both scary and exhilarating to realize

that it had been looking at her that had invoked such tenderness. She wasn't sure which emotional reaction she was more afraid of.

"My turn," she said softly. With fingers that shook, she did to Ben what he had done to her. She undressed him one step at a time. His legs were strong and sturdy, seemingly locked to the earth so that nothing could put him off balance. When she slipped his shirt from his strong shoulders, she realized he was tan all over and that well-defined muscles had barely been hinted at under his expensive clothing.

"You're so handsome," she whispered. Her fingers traced the flat expanse of his washboard stomach. "Not too much, not too little."

"Careful what you're discussing," he said with a husky laugh. "Most men would rather have too much than too little."

Her chuckle was low, soft and filled with intense desire that she couldn't hide anymore. "If I were you, I wouldn't worry about that," she said softly, exploring his body with her fingers, loving the texture of his skin under her hands.

He slipped her bra straps off and undid the fastener in one smooth motion, then bent down to peel off her panties, which ended up with the rest of her clothing. His mouth was even with her breast, and he dropped light kisses across her soft roundness and tender skin.

Her breath quickened as his tongue laved her nipple, then ran over her ribs, then dipped into her navel. His mouth continued its foray, finally sipping at the very heart of her desire. His breath came out in a long puff, warming the core of her.

Elizabeth couldn't quite believe this was happening to her. She kept her balance by holding on to his broad shoulders, but keeping a sane thought was impossible as overpowering emotions consumed every part of her.

"Ben." It sounded like a plea. Her rasping voice echoed through the bedroom as loudly as the zipper had earlier.

"Mmm?" he murmured, and the sound reverberated erotically against her skin. He clasped her buttocks, soothing, smoothing, feeding the tension he built so effortlessly in her body.

"Ben," she repeated, her head bowed as she watched the top of his dark head. This time it sounded like a prayer.

"Shh, darling," he whispered.

"Ben," she said once more, in a light whisper carried on her breath. Her fingers dug into his shoulders, her mind shut down as her body took over, revelling in the immense and wonderful pressure building inside her.

He finally rose, slowly, a smile on his mouth. Effortlessly, he swung her into his arms and laid her on the bed. And then he covered her body with his own, claiming it as his territory. He entered her easily, immediately.

He thrust once, twice, three times, and Elizabeth clung to him, reeling out of control for the first time in her life, free-falling into heaven. "Ben!" she cried.

His own body stiffened then, exploding with the same intensity that she had just experienced. A moan that came from deep within his chest sounded more like pain than ecstasy. The *petite morte.*

Ben's body went limp, and Elizabeth stroked his back and sides, loving the feel of his skin and needing to touch him.

"Ben." The word came out on a satisfied sigh that only utter completion brings.

He kissed her then, his lips warm and responsive and loving. And with that kiss it felt as if they had been together forever, a feeling so sweet she wanted to cry with the happiness of it. It was a kiss that spoke silent volumes, of thoughts, wishes, dreams, but most of all, it spoke of hopes.

She closed her eyes and, for the first time in her life, began to hope that this man would want to be with her as much as she wanted to be with him. She didn't have hopes of happily ever after; she was too realistic for that. But she did have hopes of being with him for—she swallowed hard as she tried to keep a light grasp on reality—for however long it lasted.

6

BEN LAY ON HIS SIDE naked, gently stroking Elizabeth's hair. She, too, was naked, shamelessly reveling in being next to him as dim light from her bedroom window dressed them both in moonlight and shadow.

He leaned over and gently touched her mouth with his, then gave her cheek and chin little butterfly kisses. Elizabeth remained on her back next to him, her eyes closed and a small smile barely tilting the corners of her mouth.

Though she lay quietly, she felt like a bundle of barely soothed nerves that needed—craved—his touch. She didn't dare move in case he stopped. She never wanted that to happen. Ever.

"What's going on in that beautiful, busy head of yours?" Ben asked, breaking the contented silence. "Are you feeling guilty already?"

She opened one eye and stared up at him, taking in every feature, every nuance. She closed it again and wiggled even more into the mattress. Yup, he was as handsome as ever. "Guilty? No? I'm like every other satisfied woman—thinking, dreaming, hoping. Enjoying the moment."

He chuckled. "That's good to know." Kissing her lips, he continued his exploration of her sated body. "Because I'm enjoying it, too."

His hand drifted down to stroke her flat stomach. "And what are your dreams?"

"I don't have dreams. My sister's the one with dreams," Elizabeth said with a smile.

"Which one?"

"Mary Ellen. She always dreamed. Ever since she was little. And my other sister, Virginia, was always *wishing* for something. It didn't matter what it was—she wished for it instead of wanting it."

"And what about you?"

"I was the pragmatic one," Elizabeth explained with an especially satisfied sigh as he ran his hand down the side of her hip. "Wishes and dreams were for those who had time to fritter the day away. I had hopes—far more realistic." She laughed softly. "I thought I was more honest and genuine than either of my sisters, with my nose stuck in the air and my feet firmly planted on the ground." She gave another laugh, this time aimed at herself. "I was wrong!"

"What makes you say that?"

"Virginia, who wished for the things she wanted, got them. She now owns a business and has a husband she loves who loves her. And a baby, too.

"Mary, more shy about declaring her own needs, dreamed all the time. Day and night. Now she has a solid, down–to–earth guy so she can soar like a bird in her own creative world. He's also a millionaire."

"Was the million important?" Ben asked, still stroking Elizabeth's belly and leg, occasionally taking a sip from her breast or the hollow in her shoulder or throat as he listened. She stretched, inviting his touch.

"No, the money isn't important, except they don't have to worry about it." She looked at him, noting the strength of his chin, the line of his jaw, the light in his dark eyes. "Have you ever noticed that when you don't have money, the lack of it becomes all important—consumes you? And when you have it, you don't need to think about all the petty stuff—clothing, food, rent, bounced checks, new TV, car repairs. Instead, you have time to worry about other problems—family relationships, the state of the world, what to order for dinner."

Ben laughed, a deep, rich sound that gave her goose bumps from the pure sexiness of it. "So how did you get to your goals?" he asked.

"I kidded myself. I 'hoped' I'd get into college. Then I studied like a demon. I 'hoped' I'd get to work with troubled teens. Then I made all the networking contacts I could to insure I reached that goal." Facing him, she rested her hand against his chest, where light fur tickled her palm. "In short, I did all the same stuff they did, except I used a different word."

"And what do you hope for now?"

She blinked. "I don't."

"Why?" he asked, his expression curious. "Do you think your life is over? Don't you have anything else to hope for?"

Her hand stopped its wandering as she looked up at him. Confusion dwelled in her eyes. "Well, I…"

"Don't you talk about hope to the teens who come to you?"

"Of course, I—"

"And don't you think they need to have that hope more than anything else?"

"Yes, but—"

"And isn't that what you gave Barbie and me?"

"Glad you learned something," she said, still collecting her wits. "And why are we discussing me when we should be discussing you?"

"Who said?" He kissed the tip of her nose. "No offense, Ms. Gallagher, but you could use a little of your own advice."

She relaxed, allowing her hand to drift over his body once more. "You sound like my sister."

"Which one?"

"Virginia."

He smiled a wistful smile and said the unexpected. "I wish Barbie had sisters and brothers."

"For her sake or for yours?"

"Both."

"Why?"

Ben's mouth was poised just above hers. His hands tightened on her small, rounded buttocks. "Isn't it just like a woman to need to know everything there is to know about a guy while donating as little information as possible about her own Achilles' heel?"

"Sounds more like a man to me," she said.

"Definitely a woman's remark."

"That's prejudice." Her lips brushed his with every syllable she spoke.

"That's right," he said, and then there were no

more words. His mouth took hers in possession, and for the time being, there was nothing more important than the two of them. Together.

AFTER TWO DOZEN KISSES at the doorway, Ben left in the middle of the night. Although Elizabeth missed him the moment he pulled out of the driveway, she felt as if she'd been given the gift of a lifetime.

It wasn't making love that had been the gift, although that had much to do with her mood. It was more the aftermath. Ben had stroked and teased and laughed, stroked and asked questions and talked, and laughed some more. And, of course, stroked. She couldn't have soaked up more of his touch if he'd been rain and she a desert flower.

He'd renewed her soul with his attention, fed her ego and made her feel as if she was a precious and treasured woman. Maybe Virginia was right. Maybe there was a small chance....

Even with her lack of sleep, Elizabeth still smiled all morning and barely contained the bounce in her step. Her feelings became even more buoyant when, midmorning, she received a delivery of two dozen bunches of irises, her favorite flowers. Nothing could keep happiness from dancing in her eyes.

Jamie, another one of her partners, stopped by her office and whistled. "Somebody loves you," she said with awe in her voice. Her eyes widened in envious appreciation as she stared into Elizabeth's office. There wasn't an empty surface in sight, every spare inch was covered with violet and golden flowers and rich greenery.

Elizabeth grinned widely. "Isn't it wonderful?"

Marina, too, stuck her head in the door, her arms full of case logs. "Irises. Are they for funerals or weddings?" She cocked her head and smiled at Elizabeth. "Or maybe, our partner went a little wild last night and enjoyed herself. Finally *did the deed.*"

Elizabeth took her partners' ribbing in stride, her own grin matching Marina's. "Break it up, you guys. It's just a sweet gesture from a sweet man."

Jamie's eyes widened. "A sweet man?" she repeated incredulously. "A sweet gesture?" Her eyes narrowed accusingly. "Okay, who are you and what have you done with our partner? 'Fess up or we'll sic another male on you!"

"Not another man, please!" Elizabeth begged, laughing. "One's enough, and he's very nice."

"Even one man is unusual for you. I always thought that if one came near, you'd hang him from the closest tree, just on principle." Jamie leaned over and sniffed a flower. "This guy must be special."

"He is. And as for my history with men, this isn't the best environment in which to meet them. Most of them have problems the size of Mount Saint Helens by the time they're finally dragged in here."

"I think it's marvelous, though," Marina said seriously. "He's a neat guy and I'm not sure he deserves you, but he's the only one I've ever seen come close. Besides, he's a hunk!''

Elizabeth flashed a relieved smile. "Thanks."

"When do you see him again?"

"Tonight."

"Great," Marina said. "Enjoy the heck out of it."

Jamie searched Elizabeth's face. "Happiness looks good on you."

Elizabeth grinned. "Feels good, too."

BEN TOOK HER OUT that evening and afterward they made love again.

They went out the next night, too.

Elizabeth couldn't believe her own good fortune. Ben was charming, attentive, funny, sexy. He was macho, but willing to listen.

For the next five weeks, Elizabeth walked around in a state of euphoria. Ben called once or twice a day with a joke or just to say hello. They met after work on the evenings they weren't going to be together later. She looked forward to those times, disappointed when he couldn't call or got tied up in a meeting.

Ben managed to spend the night with her on the few occasions when Barbie was visiting his mother. Those mornings, she awoke in his arms and they made slow, satisfying love in the early daylight before heading off in different directions.

She didn't know if a relationship could be truly so wonderful. But she did know she was falling in love. And she kept that secret to herself.

One Friday they had planned on going to a

movie, then returning home to a glass of wine and a night of love.

When Ben arrived to pick her up, his gaze heated her skin. Memories of the night before hung vivid and alive between them.

"You look beautiful, as usual," he murmured, holding her as close as he could get without being naked. When their lips touched, the incredible magic they made together was back.

"I bet you say that to all the women," she replied breathlessly when their kiss ended.

He smiled from the inside out and her heart flipped. She was amazed that not everyone swooned from just one of his smiling glances. He was wearing slacks and a teal colored jersey top that screamed designer and felt silky under her fingertips, which was her excuse to keep touching him.

Ben didn't seem to mind at all. "Yes, but I don't mean it when I say it to *them*," he teased. He stared at her appreciatively.

She had chosen a soft blue dress she'd found at a secondhand shop for next to nothing. But even when it was new, no designer had been willing to acknowledge the creation with a signature. It was a reminder of how far apart they were. He thought nothing of buying label clothes. It was normal for him. For the first time in her life, she wished she had at least one designer outfit.

Ben had chosen the movie—a light comedy that was witty and enjoyable. She sat with her hand on his thigh; he kept his arm around her. They shared popcorn and she ate small toffees from his hand. They laughed in all the right places and felt sad when they were supposed to.

And all the while, Elizabeth wondered about every thought going through his mind. She wondered if his attention was split between her and the screen. He squeezed her hand or stroked her shoulder occasionally. And even more often, she felt his gaze. From the corner of her eye she could see him grin at an actor's quick-witted comeback.

Feeling her eyes on him, he glanced down at her. His look changed from easygoing to heated in the space of a second. The intense connection of the moment, ignited the smoldering embers of the fire he'd built in her the night before. She suddenly wanted to be anywhere but here. Somewhere private, where she could be in his arms and leave the worries of the world behind.

His mouth briefly touched hers in a promise. "I know, love," he whispered. "I know."

Feeling the heat of a blush on her cheeks, Elizabeth turned and stared at the big screen. She hadn't realized her desire was so easily read. She felt like a young teenager on a first date, wondering if he wanted to kiss her—and if he did, what she would do. What would happen next? What should she say? The questions went on and on.

The bare-bones truth was that she wanted Ben to make love to her, to stroke her, to tell her how wonderful she was. She wanted lots more, and more again of what she experienced whenever she was in his arms.

"Tell me," he said, whispering in her ear as he covered her hand with his own.

She realized that she had a death grip on him,

her fingers digging into his thigh muscles. She was a counselor, for heaven's sake! She always told everyone to be up front and say what they needed, wanted, desired. *Stop playing games. Don't let emotion overthrow logic.* Yet here she was, watching a movie, and she couldn't for the life of her remember what was happening from one moment to the next!

All she wanted was to be alone with him, and tell him what had been on her mind for the past week, ever since she'd missed her period.

"Is everything okay?" Ben whispered when she didn't answer immediately. Now his look was concerned.

She loosened her death grip and leaned toward him. "No. I'd rather be at home, in bed with you, making mad, passionate love or staring at the ceiling and talking afterward."

"Now?" he asked, the light in his dark eyes growing even brighter.

"Now."

His mouth brushed hers, and when he pulled back he took his muscled arm from around her shoulders. He grabbed the popcorn and stood, holding her hand and pulling her out of her seat. "Excuse me," he said quietly to the couple next to them, and they moved their knees out of the way.

In five minutes he and Elizabeth were in the car, heading down the road. Elizabeth sat quietly, hands in her lap, and stared straight ahead. She couldn't believe they'd just walked out in the middle of a film. Had she *really* been so forward?

Talking about being forward and being forward were two different things.

"I'm sorry you didn't get to see the end of the movie," she murmured.

"In six months we'll rent it. But nothing will ever replace this memory." As if he'd read her mind, Ben took her hand and placed it back on his thigh. "Don't get cold feet now, darlin'," he said softly.

"I'm not. I meant what I said. I'm just surprised that I said it."

His laugh was husky. "I hope you never stop saying what's on your mind."

"You like people who speak up?"

"I like *you* to speak up."

"I've never done that before."

"Why? Aren't you supposed to have wants and needs, too?"

They pulled into the driveway. "Ben..." She was robbed of words. What she wanted most in the world to tell him—*I love you with all my heart*—she couldn't say. Even though he'd hinted that he wanted her to be open about all her feelings, she wasn't quite ready to say it aloud, and he certainly wasn't ready to hear it. Maybe later.

He palmed the keys and stared down at her as if she was taking away his birthday toy. "Don't tell me. You have a headache."

She couldn't help the smile. "No."

"Anything else to block the rest of the evening?"

"No."

"Then you haven't changed your mind?" He

looked at her with hope glimmering in his eyes. She smiled. He was playing a game, pretending he wasn't the big bad predator. But behind that innocent gaze was sheer male determination, the tough kind.

Yet he was leaving the final decision up to her. She touched his jaw. "I want you so much I can feel you inside me already. I want your smile, your caring, your loving." She smiled. "And I want it now."

His grin was slow in coming, but when it formed it lit up the inside of the car with pure, unadulterated joy. "Yes, ma'am," he said, his heated look restored.

He got out and came around to her side, opening her door and helping her out. Together they walked to the house and Elizabeth handed him the key. When he'd opened the lock, he stood aside to let her enter first.

But when they stepped inside the door, he shut it behind him with a snap. Then he turned her around and they were in each others arms, kissing as if there were no tomorrow.

Her stomach clenched with desire at just the thought of him being next to her. Inside her. She needed his mouth on hers as much as she needed air. Her hands flew everywhere, touching, stroking, kneading, tearing the designer clothes off his back.

Ben gave a low chuckle and she answered with breathless laughter. When they were naked, they clung to each other for a moment, as if they were in the middle of a whirling tornado.

Elizabeth's breath came in light gasps as she

sank to the floor. Ben followed, his gaze narrowed, his breath deep and fast, moving his chest in a way that made her want to stroke it, to feel the muscles expand and contract with his breathing. He covered her, his scent filling her nostrils, acting as the most powerful of aphrodisiacs.

Loving the feeling of being filled by him, Ben's body blended with hers until she couldn't tell the difference between her skin and his. Her fingers and his. She clung to his shoulders and waist as he entered her. He completed her. He made her feel whole and alive.

Ben's mouth sought her breast, his tongue rimming her nipple until she thought she would scream with pleasure. She arched her back, offering more. The ache was overwhelming. He showed no preference, going from one breast to the other before working his way up to her throat.

"That's it, my love. That's it," he whispered, and the sound was so erotic she held his head to her ear so he could continue. "Feel me inside."

He thrust himself into her and she thrust back, loving the feeling of being so in sync. She stroked his sides, then grasped his narrow hips with her hands as she rotated her torso against his. They were doing a dance, a ballet just for the two of them—and their rhythm was perfect. She wanted to cry at the beauty of it.

A force, a power built inside her, filling her with wonder and awe, even as she realized she was acting purely on instinct. She was a female who knew this was her mate and needed to complete the union. Her muscles clenched with the knowledge of what would happen next....

She soared, crying at the perfection of it. She clung to him, to this man who had given her such a complete and wonderful gift.

She heard his husky laughter as he watched her face, and she knew he was reading her ecstasy. Seconds later, his expression turned feral and he thrust once more, then once again, and then with a satisfied groan, collapsed next to her. He smoothed her hair back from her face as he stared down at her. Sweat tinged his brow. Absolute and utter delight lit his eyes—those eyes she loved so much.

Bending his head, he lightly, lovingly, chastely, kissed her mouth. He said two simple words that filled her heart until she thought it would burst. "Thank you."

She smiled slowly and watched him smile in turn. "You're welcome."

"Are you okay?"

"More than okay," she murmured, still not letting go of his shoulders. "I'm terrific."

Holding her hand, Ben rolled off Elizabeth's slim body to the carpeted floor next to her. "You can say that again."

"I wonder how the movie ended?"

"It was a perfect ending," he said. "The woman rode off into the sunset with the hero, and the last time anyone saw them, they were up in the mountains in the mouth of a cave, making mad passionate love on bear rugs."

"It was contemporary, and the cave floor would have been even more rough than this."

He laughed softly. "Okay. They *drove* off into the sunset and he made mad passionate love to her in the entrance of their new home."

"*Her* new home," Elizabeth corrected, rolling on her side and staring down at him.

"Poetic license."

She dropped a kiss on his mouth. "In that case, she was so enthralled with the hero that she decided to repeat the adventure." She tugged on his bottom lip with a tender bite. "This time in bed."

"I like the way you think, you sweet and wonderful heroine," he said, capturing her in his arms.

BEN STARED OUT the window at the night sky and Elizabeth's backyard. His arms were around her from behind and her hands held his against her stomach. It was a beautiful night made even more beautiful by the contentment he felt.

"A shooting star," she said, pointing up at the sky.

But Ben had already seen it. "Make a wish."

"State a hope," she said. "My sister makes the wishes."

"Okay," he said patiently. "State a hope."

She rested the back of her head against his shoulder, and he took a deep breath, smelling the sweet, clean essence of her wafting from her hair and lightly heated skin. His arms tightened around her waist.

Elizabeth closed her eyes and made a...hope. She wanted her love returned. *He loves me*, she hoped with all the intensity in her heart.

Ben cleared his throat to talk. Elizabeth brought out so many emotions in him, and they all seemed to be heightened right now. He'd never felt this happy. "What did you hope for?" he asked.

She smiled. "Can't tell or it won't come true."

He tightened his arms around her. "I thought you told me you don't believe in that stuff."

"I don't. But you don't deliberately put a jinx on it, just in case...."

Ben laughed. "I see. Hedging your bets."

"Not at all," she countered, feeling the tiniest bit defensive. "I prefer to think of it as being cautious."

"Be cautious and tell me anyway."

She smiled. "Are you sure you want to hear the truth?"

"I'm sure."

She took a deep breath and slowly let it out. Turning in his arms, she reached up and planted a light kiss on his mouth, then followed with several little kisses on the strong column of his throat and under his ear.

Her gaze delved into his. "I love you, Ben Damati. I love you with all my heart and soul. And I wished—hoped—that you love me." There it was. It was out. The feeling was almost euphoric, and very scary.

His laugh turned to a growl that came from deep in his chest. Then the growl disappeared as his expression slowly changed from indulgent to...closed.

It startled her. "Are you okay?"

With his brows raised, his smile indulgent, he said, "Sure. Are you?" False.

"I'm wonderful," she said, pretending she wasn't hurt by him ignoring her declaration. Silently, she prayed he would say something. Anything. Something that would tell her he was half as much in love as she was.

She looked into his eyes and saw...nothing.

"I can tell that just by looking at you," he countered in a teasing tone, but the words sounded hollow. "I bet you were wonderful as a child, too." It was said by rote, without meaning. Raising his arm, he glanced at his wrist. A dark brown alligator band accented a cream-faced gold watch. Another watch. Most people had one. He had half a dozen.

Elizabeth said the only thing on her mind that wouldn't cost her any more hurt than what was already branding her soul. "Beautiful watch."

"Thanks. It was a gift."

She didn't ask from whom. When he used that softer, kinder tone of voice, it usually had something to do with his wife.

Suddenly he looked as if he was full of energy. He gave her forehead a quick kiss. "I hate to make love and run, but I promised Barbie I'd be home early." Suddenly, he was slipping into his clothing as if it was the most natural thing in the world.

It wasn't natural. She'd just declared—for the first time in her life—that she was in love with the man whose arms were around her, holding her.

And he hadn't responded.

Or rather, he had. He'd deliberately ignored her declaration. He didn't love her. He didn't want to hear about her loving him.

She felt an embarrassed blush spread from the soles of her feet to the top of her head. She wanted to dig a hole and jump in. Instead, she was standing in the middle of her bedroom, naked, while Ben stood there dressed. It was terribly wrong.

He was supposed to be spending the night. They'd agreed days ago.

Instead of the euphoric feeling of just a few minutes ago, she now felt as if she'd been used. As if she were slightly damaged goods. Yet she couldn't put a finger on what had just happened. She had turned him off just by uttering words of love. So much for truth and justice.

Elizabeth wrapped the soft, peach-colored bed sheet around her body like a toga. "We wouldn't be home from the movie yet," she said quietly.

"Then I have a head start," he answered offhandedly, tucking in his shirt and looking as if he couldn't run out the door quickly enough. "I'll call you tomorrow and set up a time we can get together this weekend." He bent toward her to kiss her on the cheek. She moved her head and kissed him on the mouth. The kiss was over in a second. No lingering. No touching. No hug.

It was a pretense of a kiss. Ben's emotions had clicked off as easily as they had clicked on earlier.

She faced him and took her courage in her hands. "You were supposed to stay. What happened, Ben? Was it because I said I love you?"

He smiled. "Of course not." He gave her a

quick peck on the forehead before turning away. "It just took me by surprise, that's all." He shrugged. "But that's not why I have to leave. Barbie isn't spending the night with Mom, after all. So I need to be in tonight. Sorry."

It was a lie. She knew it. He knew it, she was sure. "Fine," she managed to say. Her words sounded as tight and stiff as she felt. "Maybe next time." Her soul shriveled with each word.

She turned and stared out the window, not wanting him to see the needy expression she was certain glowed in her eyes. Fragile ego that she had, she needed some kind of reassurance that they were still together. A pair. A couple. She needed encouragement so she would be strong enough to continue in this relationship knowing that he didn't love her while she loved him with all her heart. Being with Ben Damati wasn't the lark her partners and relatives had suggested. It was real. As real as her broken heart. Ben's approval was necessary to her. So was his love. She'd wanted to hear a repeat of what was in her own heart, but instead he'd withdrawn instantly.

Now she wanted him out the door before she cried buckets from the hurt, imaginary or otherwise. She was so embarrassed she wanted to disappear into the woodwork.

"Elizabeth," he said, catching her attention.

She pretended she was looking at the dark yard. "Yes?"

"Elizabeth Jean." His voice was soft but insistent.

Forcing her best smile, she turned her head and looked at him. He stood on the other side of the bed, hands in his pockets. He was the love of her life—and suddenly so out of reach. That was apparent immediately. She should have known she couldn't change the order of things. "Yes?"

"Aren't you going to walk me to the door?"

Her smile became more brilliant and she tried to sound as if she was teasing. "You know where it is, don't you?"

His gaze narrowed and he looked thoughtful. Or was it guilty? "Are you okay?" he asked.

She gave a short laugh. "Of course." As if this scene was played out every day of her life.

"I'll pick you up tomorrow about seven-thirty, okay?" His voice had changed to a softer, more loving tone, but the damage was done. The distance between them right now was too awesome to bridge.

"For what?" she asked, turning to stare out the window again.

"Dinner," he reminded her. "You already accepted. I told Barbie and she asked if she could come along. I told her I'd let her know tonight."

Elizabeth swallowed her pride. "Of course. I think that's a great idea."

"Seven-thirty. Right?"

He sounded indecisive, but the thought of him staying now was impossible to bear. She wasn't fool enough to believe he'd suddenly declare his love. She knew better than that. If it was going to happen, it would have already.

He had to leave now, while she still had command of her emotions. "Right. Give Barbie a hug for me when you get home. Tell her I'm looking forward to tomorrow." She turned, her bright smile in place once more. "Now get, before Barbie falls asleep."

A quick look of relief crossed his face before he smiled. "Thanks. See you then."

His footsteps echoed down the hall until he hit the carpeting. A moment later she heard the door open, then quietly close. Two minutes later she heard his engine rev and the sound of his car pulling out of the drive. And then he was gone.

Only then did she let down her guard. One tear followed another down her cheeks.

Ben had gotten just what he wanted. He'd enjoyed the chase and earned his reward: Elizabeth in bed, making passionate love beyond anything she'd ever envisioned in a lifetime.

With the movements of an old woman, she sat on the edge of the bed and wiped her tears away. Then she cried again for what could have been.

She had made the mistake of believing he had wanted to hear her tell the truth of her love. That maybe then she could share with him her growing suspicions that she might be pregnant. Ben hadn't been ready. He hadn't really wanted to hear what she had to say. In fact, he wanted to run as far and as fast as he could from her, or he wouldn't have left at all.

But it wasn't irreversible, she told herself, clinging to hope. He might think about it and realize just how much he loved her in return. And he did, didn't he? All this time spent together couldn't have been just because she was nice to be with. He had to have felt something deeper. He wasn't that heartless. She wasn't that wrong about him....

She wiped away another tear. Her hurt and misery were slowly hardening into anger. He'd asked for the truth and got it. Then he'd decided he didn't like it. Well, that was okay, too! If he didn't want to be a part of her life, she would survive, she told herself. She had always been single, so she hadn't lost a thing. Instead, she'd gained experience that would make her a better, wiser woman.

And then she lay down, curled into a ball and cried herself to sleep.

BEN TURNED off the highway onto a country road. He needed to clear the cobwebs from his mind and figure out just what all these thoughts hammering at him meant.

He had just made wonderful, passionate love to a woman he'd never dreamed he'd find. One who was deserving of kindness and honesty and all the sweetness life could offer.

Someone who loved him with all her heart. He'd known that even before she'd spoken; he'd seen it in her eyes. He'd known it and ignored it, thinking, hoping she would never have the nerve to voice her feelings aloud. He'd been wrong.

And instead of feeling the awe and wonder she obviously felt, he'd felt constricted and out of breath. Suddenly, from being the happiest, most contented he'd ever been, he was dying to get away and take deep, gulping breaths of fresh air.

He'd wanted to run and hide, to get out of Elizabeth's home. To get away from Elizabeth herself.

He had looked down at her beautiful face and

suddenly, without warning, had seen the all-encompassing love there. And he'd felt trapped.

One minute he couldn't get enough of her, the next he was afraid to stay with her a moment longer. His greatest fear was to get caught in a set of circumstances that would be out of his control.

Until tonight, he'd been the one doing the pursuing, not Elizabeth. He had chased her all the way. He'd pressed for her attention, solicited her appreciation and practically begged for her favors. He'd done everything he knew to make her fall in love with him, but until five weeks ago, she'd been a reluctant date. There was no doubt in his mind that she didn't jump into *anyone's* bed easily.

And, damn it, he was an honorable man. He wouldn't have taken her to bed and made love to her if he hadn't been. He treated all the women in his past with respect and dignity, and he made sure he didn't get involved unless he was very interested in the first place. Elizabeth, like every other woman he'd been with, had had the opportunity to turn his offer down. Not one woman had. In the end, he and whoever had parted amicably and gone their separate ways.

Obviously, it wouldn't be like that with Elizabeth.

She was so very different.

Which explained his blind fear and panic.

He'd pursued her, won her and got exactly what he wanted. And then he'd run like hell.

He was ashamed of himself.

But when she'd turned and gazed out the window so she wouldn't have to look at him, he'd stared at her back. With her creamy skin wrapped in that pale peach sheet, she had never looked so vulnerable. Physically, he'd been ready to carry her back to bed and treasure her in his arms for the rest of the night. But when he saw her face reflected in the glass, he realized she was on the verge of tears. Tears she would shed because of him.

And he'd wanted to run away.

He felt like a heel. But, hell, the truth was he'd felt trapped.

He didn't believe in love, although everyone said it was real. Maybe it was some flaw in his genetic makeup that made it impossible for him to commit himself totally. Maybe he hadn't met the right woman. Maybe it wasn't possible for men in general.

All he knew was that he wouldn't spend the rest of his life with a woman and not have whatever that feeling was. If he never married again, because he didn't feel "love," then so be it.

Besides, Elizabeth deserved more, too.

Frustration filled him to the brim. Damn it! The worst drunks could fall in love. The wealthiest old men in the world could fall in love. Why couldn't he?

In his marriage he might not have had love, but he had freedom. He'd lived his life passing her in halls, in kitchens, at tables, and had had her in his bed when he wanted her. They'd lived in the same house, but they hadn't lived *together*. At first, it was okay, but slowly it turned into a misery neither of them fully realized because it happened so gradually. Like getting used to the fires of hell by upping the temperature a little at a time.

He didn't want that kind of life again—couldn't face that emotional emptiness of waiting for the god of love to shoot an arrow into his heart and make him feel whole. He refused to let himself fall in that well again.

Ben hit the steering wheel with his fist, enduring the pain because it was nothing compared to what was going on inside him. Exhausted from his mental gymnastics, he turned the car around and drove home.

Maybe by the time he saw Elizabeth again, this heart-pounding, breathtaking, panicked feeling that resounded through every muscle of his body would be gone.

Something deep inside told him he was kidding himself....

7

ELIZABETH HAD MORE THAN one problem on her plate, and she wasn't sure about anything. She told herself that Ben was under pressure, what with Barbie and his business. As a therapist, she knew that such stress caused many people to withdraw. Although people's problems might vary, their reactions were usually textbook. Fear triggered one of two reactions: fight or flight. Aggression or retreat.

Ben had retreated into himself. She told herself that once he got home and made sure that his baby—even though she was a teenager—was all right, his fears would abate.

After rationalizing all this, she prayed she was right.

When Ben arrived to pick her up for dinner Saturday night, he was easygoing and friendly. His kiss was light and his eyes danced with wicked sensuality.

It would be okay. She felt warm and special, almost glowing under his intimate gaze. Their second kiss was long, slow and every bit as wonderful as anything she'd imagined in her dreams.

But within the hour, his wall was back in place, and he was as distant as he'd been the night before.

They ate at one of the finer seafood restaurants because shrimp was Barbie's favorite. The more Ben retreated, the more confused and hurt Elizabeth felt. By the middle of the dinner, she was so on edge it was all she could do to keep her attention on what the young girl was saying.

Seemingly relaxed and casual, Ben leaned back in his chair and listened with rapt attention to his daughter as she talked to Elizabeth about school and friends.

"...And I told Angie I was an honor roll student to begin with, so I'm helping her catch up with her biology notes." Barbie looked pensive for a moment. "With only twelve of us in school, we get to talk. It could be, like, lots worse."

"You're also doing well because you're making the best of it," Elizabeth said encouragingly. "You should be proud of yourself for handling the change so well, Barbie."

The teen looked as if Elizabeth had just handed her a rose. "Thanks. One of the girls' dad is out of a job. He had a janitor service that went belly up, and he's miserable. He's been everywhere trying to find a job, and hasn't yet. She says it's too tough at home to be able to find some way to get through this. She's giving up the baby and wishes it was soon, because her family just doesn't have any money."

"There's nothing wrong with that decision, Barbie," Elizabeth said gently. She heard her own words and, for the first time, realized just what they meant. She had her own problems. Doubts. Fears. Her gaze darted to Ben, but he didn't return her look.

"There is when money is the only reason for giving up your very own baby," the young girl argued, her expression immediately turning stubborn and haughty.

"It's a good reason to give up a child," Elizabeth corrected, unwilling to let Barbie lose that option. "If that's what's best for baby and biological mother."

Ben took a sip of his iced tea. "Grab one of my business cards, take it with you tomorrow and ask your friend's dad to give me a call. I think I might be able to help."

Barbie's blue eyes lit up. "Really, Daddy?"

Elizabeth watched the two interact. Ben was trying so hard to connect. It was a shame he refused to do the same with her. As quickly as he'd turned on the charm, he'd turned it off.

She listened with one ear, her attention riveted on Ben as his lips moved to form words. His mouth was like a carefully sculpted piece of art. That sexy mouth had kissed her in places no one else had ever explored. Had held her captive, had made love to her. That mouth had been as passionate as the man, as wondrous as his touch.

Heat flashed down her spine and turned her legs to lead. She held her breath until the sensation passed. Acknowledging his attraction and her own love was okay, she told herself. But it was *not* okay to relive those emotions at the dinner table.

Ben gave her an odd glance, and she raised her brows in a silent dare. He looked away.

"Have you decided what you're going to do about the father of my grandchild?" Ben finally asked Barbie, clearly distracted by Elizabeth's expression but determined to get on with his own agenda.

Barbie sent him a look that spoke volumes. "No. And it's none of your business, Daddy."

"Of course it is," he answered evenly. "Don't you think the other set of grandparents deserve to know their grandchild?"

"No."

But Ben wasn't about to give up. "I deserve to have a talk with the young man responsible for this."

"I know you," she said, her young voice rising with each word. "You'd blow it all out of proportion."

His eyes widened in disbelief. "My daughter's a teenager, pregnant, not married and won't acknowledge the father, and I'd *blow it out of proportion?*"

Barbie's blue eyes shot fire.

"I think Barbie needs to finish the rest of her dinner—and milk." Elizabeth said calmly. "That would be the best next step."

The young girl sent her a thankful look that wasn't wasted on her father.

"Whose side are you on?" Ben demanded, his irritation barely leashed.

Elizabeth stared back. "Mine. I came to enjoy my dinner and the company," she stated calmly, even while her stomach churned. "I didn't come to referee the great debate."

That was enough to silence everyone.

But at that moment, Elizabeth realized she'd lost him. As if she'd ever had him. Her love for him didn't really matter. He didn't feel the same way.

They all shared a huge ice cream sundae for dessert.

Conversation slowly returned, easing some of the wire-tight tension. But it didn't disappear altogether.

Ben dropped Barbie by their house with an admonition to get to bed early, then drove Elizabeth home. They rode in silence, letting the soft music of a compact disc fill the void.

Her tension had escalated to strain by the time they reached her driveway. Ben was still frowning and being distant. She didn't know where to begin or exactly what to say, and dreaded sharing her unexpected news with him. The last two days of her body's antics had made earlier suspicions turn into an "almost fact." Especially since the night before, when her stomach tensed with every thought.

She wanted to talk to him privately, tell him what she thought, sound him out on being a father for the second time. But her nerve deserted her. The only good thing about being a therapist was that she knew how to justify being a coward. Stress wasn't good at this time. She'd wait for another time.

What chance do you have to keep this a secret, girl? she asked herself, knowing she was only putting off the inevitable. Still, she hesitated....

She took a deep breath and plunged in before she lost her nerve. "Would you come in for a glass of wine?"

He gave her a hint of a smile and turned off the

car engine. "I'd love to. There's something I need to ask you. Maybe you can help me out."

Elizabeth's heart raced as she led the way to the kitchen and poured two glasses of red wine into her best crystals, knowing she wouldn't be drinking hers. Maybe her news would let them go back to the easy, special relationship they'd had until now. Maybe whatever was bothering him would disappear and they could love each other the way she'd hoped they would. She needed that more than breathing. He'd shown her what heaven was like and she wanted more. She wanted to live with her love and raise a bunch of little loves. She wanted to be with him early in the morning and curl up next to him late at night.

One look at his frowning expression shot down her hope. Maybe pigs would fly.

She handed him a glass of ruby-red merlot, then sat on the couch and waited for him to join her. He did, but he was slow about it.

"What's your question?" Elizabeth asked as casually as she could manage. Hope was hard to tamp down; it wanted to spread through her limbs and warm her heart.

Ben stared into his wine for a moment before looking back up at her. His gaze was hard and purposeful. Determined. "I'm thinking of hiring a private detective to find the young man who did this to Barbie."

It wasn't the problem Elizabeth wanted to address, but it was obviously the primary one on his mind. "And what will that solve?" she asked.

"It will make me feel a whole hell of a lot better," he stated grimly. "It's about time he did his growing up, too."

"It will also insure that Barbie doesn't talk to you for a long time to come."

"She'll realize I did the right thing. Secretly, I think she wants me to take the bull by the horns and expose him for what he is."

"My foot!" Elizabeth declared. "If she wanted you to do this, Ben, she would have dropped more clues so he could be 'accidentally' found out. But she hasn't."

His jaw clenched. "It's a chance I have to take."

But his anger wasn't enough of a deterrent to keep Elizabeth quiet. She couldn't let him do something so damaging to his relationship with Barbie without trying to stop him. "And as for exposing him for what he is—well, I think we already know what he is. He's a sixteen-year-old kid who's scared his plans in life will go up in smoke. He can run away from this and no one will know. Barbie can't do that until the baby is born."

"It's damn unfair that she has to go through this alone!" Ben's anger filled the air with tension. He was at the breaking point and it showed. "He should be made to suffer as much as she is."

"First of all, she's not going through it alone. She's got you, Marina, her friends and me."

"But not him."

"Not him," Elizabeth repeated firmly. "I think you're obsessing about the boy instead of honing in on Barbie's problems. I just don't understand why."

Ben placed his untouched glass on the coffee table and stood. With his hands in his pockets, he walked to the window and stared out at the dark night sky. Elizabeth watched and waited quietly, praying with all her might that she'd hear something that would make her understand his withdrawal from her.

"I was a dumb nineteen-year-old college kid when Jeanne told me she was pregnant."

Elizabeth's heart sank. Suddenly, she understood his reluctance to discuss his wife in more personal terms. His reluctance to commit. His reluctance to love. And in understanding, she knew her own love was doomed. "And you did what was expected and married her. You did what was *right*."

"Yes." He looked at her over his shoulder, his eyes confirming her words even before she said them. "I was a man about it. I didn't dishonor either one of us."

"And you think Barbie's young man should come forward and offer Barbie the same thing? Put himself in the same place?"

"No, of course not." Ben came back to the couch and sat down. "I don't want Barbie to feel she has to marry the guy. I want this jerk to know that he has a responsibility and that it's Barbie's choice to let him off the hook. He should realize he didn't get away with anything."

"That will punish him?"

"That will teach him to keep his pants zipped," Ben corrected.

"And pay child support," she guessed.

"You're damn right."

"What did you do?"

His anger filled the room. "I worked for two, went to school for two, prayed our lives would get better, and made things happen. And that's what he should be doing."

"Is that what this is really all about, Ben?" Elizabeth asked softly. Tears welled in her eyes, but she refused to lose control and let them fall. She was understanding now what had happened to them and what the future would be like when she told him her news. His feelings wouldn't change. He'd want to do the honorable thing. Whether it was right or not.

Whether he loved her or not.

She couldn't do that. There was too much at stake. Then a realization flashed through her mind and her eyes widened with the simplicity of it. "Or is it that this young man proved you couldn't protect Barbie from all the bad things in the world? Just like you couldn't protect your wife from cancer?" Elizabeth was just guessing, but his anger was now making sense.

Ben's head snapped up, his gaze as cold and chilling as a Nordic wind. "That's not true."

"What *is* true?" she asked, knowing she understood him for the very first time. "This young man not only competed with you for your daughter's attention—and won—he also showed you how you'd failed, in your own mind, to protect your family." She watched the expressions flitting over his face. "Again."

Ben stood, his dark gaze locking with hers. Anger emanated from him as if it was a tangible, physical thing. It frightened her, but she refused to look away.

Like a bolt out of the blue, she realized how attuned she was to his every move. He could bring her to tears so easily. But that wasn't unusual. After all, Elizabeth Jean Gallagher was in love with Ben Damati. She loved him with all her heart and soul. She was willing to fight for their love, but wasn't willing to stand by and keep her mouth shut while Ben continued to make the same mistakes that had brought him to this point of misery.

When he finally spoke, his voice was cold and rough. "Well, Ms. Psychologist, you're way out of your league. You don't need to analyze me. You were hired to do that for my daughter, and you turned her over to someone else."

Her head snapped back as if he'd struck her a physical blow. His words were meant to wound, and they did. His anger was like another person standing between them.

Swallowing hard to keep her dry throat from closing completely, Elizabeth stood up in turn. "Don't aim your anger at me, Ben. I'm just the messenger."

"You don't know what the hell you are," he growled, striding toward her. His hands circled her arms as if he wanted to restrain her, but his grip was light. "I'll take care of my own—and in my own way."

"You're making a mistake," she said evenly. Her heart was breaking and still she tried to keep a handle on reason. She couldn't let it go without one more try. "This is Barbie's decision. Not yours."

His brows rose, daring her to approach him with her philosophy once more. "I don't think so." He let go of her arms, walked to the door and gave her one more angry glare. "It's just as well. You'd eat a man for lunch before you'd admit you might be wrong."

"Because I speak my mind?" she demanded.

"Because you don't have room in your life for any ego besides your own."

She wanted to make a cutting retort, or cry, but it was too late. Ben was out the door and down the drive before she could find the voice to throw out her last dart, and by that time it was too late. "You're a rough work in progress, Ben Damati," she whispered to the empty room. "And the father of our child."

THREE DAYS LATER, Elizabeth stood in front of the kitchen phone staring at it. She had not spoken to Ben since their ill-fated dinner. She'd never told him her news. It was going to take every ounce of nerve she had to make this phone call. But it was necessary. Ben had a right to know.

After taking a deep breath, she picked up the receiver and dialed his number. The answering machine picked up and she was relieved. It postponed the inevitable. "Hi, Ben. It's Elizabeth. Please give me a call to set up a time I can see you. I need to tell you something in private."

When she hung up the phone, she was shaking.

There was no doubt about it. She was pregnant.

Her doctor had called and confirmed her condition at four o'clock that afternoon. She had suspected but she hadn't known for certain. Now that it was fact, she was in shock. She could hardly think, barely talk. Being single and pregnant was against everything she'd ever taught or believed. Every child deserved two parents, if that was possible. And deserved to know it was wanted....

What could she do?

Ben had been trapped into marriage once by an unplanned pregnancy. As much as Elizabeth hoped she would be with Ben for the rest of her life, she knew by his actions in the past weeks that hers was nothing but a pipe dream. He had to love her for their relationship to work. He couldn't feel trapped again, or they both would wind up losers. Without love, they didn't stand a chance at happiness.

If there had been any hope for them, this ended it.

She sat for half an hour and stared at the walls. She had to take care of herself, stay calm, eat the right foods. And be prepared for the changes that her life would undergo. Her body had to make a warm nest for their child.

So many changes. But one big one stood out like a beacon in the night. She was going to be a mother....

When the doorbell rang, she jumped.

From the front doorstep, Ben looked at her as if he was seeing a stranger. In silence, he stepped in and Elizabeth led him into the kitchen and poured him a cup of coffee. She dreaded the next twenty minutes. When he finally spoke, it was in a soft voice as if he realized she was under strain. "I picked up the messages from the car and was just a couple of blocks from your house. What's the matter?"

She wished she could be anywhere but here. "Ben," she said, sitting down across from him and placing her hands on the table. "I'm pregnant."

Ben's gaze narrowed, searching her face for confirmation of the words. "And I'm the father." It wasn't a question.

"Yes."

He closed his eyes. Elizabeth waited. It had been a shock to her, but she'd had a growing suspicion. For him, this was coming out of the blue. He needed time to adjust.

He opened his eyes and focused back on her. "What do you want to do?"

"I want to have the baby."

He stood, his body rigid with determination. "We'll get married." His decision had been made. "Next week. I'll make the arrangements." He turned as if to leave. "Let me know if you need something. Meanwhile, I'll be back tomorrow."

"No."

Her voice was soft, but it stopped him in his tracks. He turned around and stared at her as if she'd spoken gibberish. "What do you mean?"

"We're not getting married." Her voice shook,

but the words were clearly stated. "We're not going to make two wrongs out of one."

Hands on his hips, his suit jacket open, he stared at her defiantly. He looked as sexy as a male cover model and as deadly as any Clint Eastwood character. "You're pregnant, I'm responsible. We're marrying. What's so hard about that?"

"That's your decision. Not mine. I'm not marrying anyone without love and you're not in love with me."

"It's the baby that's important here. You've said so yourself, to both me and Barbie." His distant look hurt so badly. "Or are you above taking your own advice?"

"No. But Barbie's situation doesn't apply here." Unwilling to give up quite yet, Elizabeth braced her hands on the table. "I'm much older and I can take care of myself. I want you in our child's life, but I'm not going to marry you to make it happen. Our child needs two happy parents, not one sad and one unhappy. And that's what we'd be if you were forced into marriage, again."

"Ever the therapist," Ben stated derisively. "Why can't you accept my decision and let it go at that?"

Her heart was breaking into tiny pieces and littering her soul. "Because I'm a person, too. I also have wants, needs and feelings. Obviously, Mr. Damati, they don't correspond with yours." Tears were pushing at her eyes, but she refused to back down.

Ben glanced at his watch. "Look, I'm on my

way to an appointment I've already broken once. I'll be back here tomorrow and we can discuss this further. Meanwhile, know that whatever happens, we'll marry to make it right. This baby will be taken care of by its father. This baby is mine!" He walked around the table and stood in front of her. His hand covered her slight tummy. His dark eyes blazed with determination. "This life is mine. I helped create it, Elizabeth. I'll be its father in every sense of the word. I've never shirked my responsibilities. I'm not going to start now."

His mouth came down and branded her with a kiss that was full of both anger and determination. Her heart skipped a beat, then her blood began roaring in her ears. When he finally pulled away, his dark eyes seared into hers. "I'll be back later."

"This baby is ours," she whispered, still defiant in the face of his overbearing attitude. "Not yours alone."

"Whatever you want to call it," he said with a wave of his hand. "Just know that I demand marriage. I don't care how. Arrange it anyway you want and I'll agree. Just as long as it's done."

He left the house as quickly as he had come.

Elizabeth sat back down in the chair and felt the blood drain from her face.

It was done.

She'd told him.

Ben knew.

And now he was willing to marry her. Just like Jeanne. It was a repeat performance he'd never wanted to make.

Marriage was the exact wrong thing to do, but at least one of them was sane. Because, despite his arrogant orders, Elizabeth realized that getting married was the worst thing they could do. Ben hadn't wanted to marry her when there was no baby or he wouldn't have pulled away emotionally. If that was the case, he certainly wouldn't want marriage any more now that she was pregnant.

But, being the stubborn man he was, he was determined to push both of them into a commitment because he thought it was the right thing to do. What a disaster. For the second time in his life, Ben was trapped. If they went through with this farce of a marriage, it would strain their relationship for the rest of their lives. Elizabeth would be the cause of his unhappiness and soon would be unhappy and unloved herself, clinging to Ben and their child because she wouldn't know what else to do.

She wanted more out of life.

Despair filled her with dread that seemed to seep into her bones, creating a cold chill that would never go away. She had never felt so alone. Just like most women who found themselves in this position, Elizabeth had no one to rely on but herself.

Tears quietly streamed down her cheeks as she stared at the wall. She didn't have time for tears, she told herself. She had to decide what to do next. She placed her hand protectively over her stomach. She had a baby to prepare for. So, until she decided what her next step should be, until she had a plan, she would remain where she was.

"IT'S BEEN TWO MONTHS since you told him and he hasn't let up yet?" Marina asked, her tone incredulous. "That's awful. What about Barbie? Have you seen her?"

Although Ben hadn't let a day pass without getting in touch, it had been the loneliest two months of Elizabeth's life. She sat behind her messy desk and looked at Marina, who was perched on the chair facing her. Having just finished a session with Ben and Barbie, Marina had burst in to demand unabashedly why Ben had to ask *her* how Elizabeth was.

"I see Barbie, occasionally, for lunch." Elizabeth didn't mention the nights she saw Ben in her dreams, walking into her office and saying something warm and wonderful. She didn't mention how awful and bleak her life looked. Or how every evening was an exercise in futility as she watched Ben pace and demand that she marry him. Or how withdrawn and abrupt he was when she refused. Or how so tired she was of fighting both him and herself. "Once in a while Barbie drives over and visits for a while."

"You must have lots of phone conversations, too, if her quotes of your wisdom are any indication," Marina observed. But she wasn't to be sidetracked. "Did you see the piece on Ben on TV?"

A leading station in Atlanta had done a piece on prisons from the eighteenth century to the present, and Ben had been one of the experts interviewed. In fact, the moderator had relied heavily on him and two senators to explain pending changes to the penal code and how they affected all types of prisons. Elizabeth had avidly watched, amazed at his expertise and his ease on camera.

"It was good, wasn't it?" she replied, knowing her voice had a ring of pride in it.

"It was great. But what's happening between you two?"

Elizabeth stared at her desk blotter for a moment before she could find her voice—the one that wouldn't break at the mention of his name. "Ben decided he didn't like my solution—which is two independent people joining together to raise a child. He's insisting on marriage. I'm still saying no."

"Why?"

Slowly, haltingly, Elizabeth told her about Ben's first marriage. She kept her explanation brief and to the point, as if she was doing a case report.

"Wow. He must have some big-time issues he's not dealing with." Marina sat back, her eyes wide. "I'm amazed. He seems so calm and easygoing. And logical! To say nothing of his good looks and personality."

"Just not with me." She kept her hands in her lap, unwilling to let her partner see that her nails were bitten to the quick. "Has he found the young man yet?"

"It's not confirmed. The P.I. he hired last month said it was probably one of two boys. Ben wants to be sure before he confronts anyone."

"Maybe he won't know for sure until the kid comes forward," Elizabeth said.

"I assume Barbie knows what the detective is doing?"

"Barbie won't discuss it with her father," Elizabeth said tiredly, pushing a strand of auburn hair behind her ear. She knew she looked as exhausted as she felt.

Marina furrowed her brow. "Barbie won't discuss it with me, either."

"Barbie told me she ran into the boy at the dentist's office a few days ago. It's the first time she's seen him since she left her regular school. She said he was stunned when he saw her belly." Elizabeth gave a mirthless laugh. "It seems that, although he knew she was having a baby, he didn't realize what 'pregnant' looked like."

"Eight months along on a small girl is big."

"Eight months on anyone is big," Elizabeth countered, curling her arms around her own stomach. "Barbie is no exception."

Marina focused a narrow gaze on her partner. "You look like you've been rode hard and put away wet," she said. "When was your last doctor's visit?"

Elizabeth gave a quick, humorless smile. "Last week," she said. "Everything is fine."

"Ben should be helping you to carry the emotional burden, Elizabeth."

"This pregnancy is mine," Elizabeth said, her expression determined. "Once the news is out, my career will be ruined, or at least on hold for a while. No one will want to send their troubled teenager to me for counseling and I don't blame them. I'm not exactly a shining example of responsible behavior."

"There are other cases you can handle until clients realize you have even more to contribute *because* of your situation. You know what it's like firsthand."

"Let's hope—" Elizabeth broke off, when a tall, very thin youth appeared in her office doorway. He wore an expression that was somewhere between stark terror and relief.

"Miss Gallagher?" he asked, his voice breaking on the last syllable. He looked from one woman to the other.

"That's me," Elizabeth said.

"Uh, Barbie Damati said you'd talk to me," he finally admitted, his face turning dark red. "She said you'd help me out."

Elizabeth's heart skipped a beat. "Are you the young man she was dating?"

Apparently, confessing was very hard and the boy struggled to get the words out. Finally, the truth burst forth. "Yes, ma'am, I am. My name is Steve Bennington."

Marina stood and held out her hand, a wide grin on her face. "Hi, there, Steve. I'm Marina, Barbie's counselor. I'm very glad to meet you." She shook his hand, not letting go right away. "I also want to tell you how proud you can feel for coming forward."

"Thanks," he said, looking a little dazed. "My parents don't know I'm here."

"Don't worry," she said softly. "It's not *our* place to tell them."

The boy looked so relieved, Elizabeth thought he was going to faint.

Marina slipped out of the office, saying, "Talk to you later," and disappeared down the hall.

Elizabeth motioned to the now-empty chair and smiled. "Sit down and let's talk," she said, thinking that her own problems might not be solvable, but at least Barbie's world held a ray of hope.

ONE WEEK LATER, with the help of Marina, Elizabeth set up a meeting between an angry Ben and a scared Steve. She hoped that Ben would temper his anger when he saw the young man, but she wasn't going to put all her pennies in that purse.

When Ben arrived, he was impeccably dressed and as charming as ever, but his face was drawn and tired. His dark eyes were just as magnetic, just as mesmerizing as always, but not when he looked at her.

"Hello, Elizabeth. How are you feeling?"

This was the first week he hadn't come over to badger her, and while she'd heaved a sigh of relief, she also missed him. She drank in the sight of him. "Hi, Ben. How are you?"

"Fine." With that dark, intense gaze she remembered so well, he looked her up and down as she stood behind her desk. Her body warmed, responded to the momentary heat of his eyes. "It looks like my absence from your life agrees with you. You've gained some weight."

"Yes." She was thankful her voice sounded ordinary and calm as she waved toward one of two chairs facing her desk. "I hope you don't mind my being here, but both Steven and Barbie asked me, and I said yes."

His expression turned grim. "So you've already met the twerp. What do you think?"

She made a point of calling the boy by his name. "Of Steven?" At Ben's impatient nod, she continued. "I think he's a scared and confused young man who's not certain about the right course to take. Just by being here, he's going against everything his parents taught him."

Ben didn't seem to care. "He deserves to be horsewhipped."

Her chin tilted. "Who made you judge and jury?"

He raised a cold brow. "Me."

She felt her frustration level rising again and tamped it down. "What is it you want him to pay for?" she asked. "Getting Barbie pregnant? Walking away? Or not coming forward earlier? Which is it?"

Ben answered quickly. "All of it." But the look on her face must have made him realize just how childish he sounded. He ran a hand around his muscled neck. "Damn it! He took my daughter without thinking of the consequences of his actions."

She didn't say the obvious: *You did the same thing to me!* "Well, he's here now."

"And so am I. Let's get down to business."

"This isn't a business deal, Ben." Elizabeth tried one more time. "Cut the boy a little slack."

"Okay, okay," he answered, his tone as weary as she felt.

One second later, a very scared Steve walked into the room, his eyes as wide as the doorway. When he shook Elizabeth's hand, she felt him trembling. Her heart went out to him. Ben had to forgive this boy or he'd never forgive himself.

She watched both closely. After he'd faced the boy, Ben's tension seemed to wane.

Marina entered and began mediating for them both. Elizabeth remained a silent presence.

They started to talk, Steve explaining his fears. Ben forced himself to listen. Before Steve came forward, it had been easy to be angry with the boy. But now, meeting with a young man who had barely left boyhood behind, anger didn't seem so appropriate.

They talked about issues that mattered. That was the first step. Elizabeth wished she could say the same thing about Ben and herself.

Finally, the meeting was over and Steven and Marina left. Nothing had been decided, but lots of issues had been aired. That was progress.

As if all his energy was gone, Ben placed his forearms on his thighs and hung his head. He rubbed the back of his neck to ease the tension he must have felt so strongly. "That was harder than I thought it was going to be."

"It went well," she said quietly.

Ben looked up, his gaze haunted. "He's just a kid, for God's sake. He's two months younger than Barbie!"

"Yes."

The room was silent for a long time before Ben spoke again. "You were quiet," he said, and it sounded like an accusation.

She felt as if she were under a microscope. "You did fine without me," she said in a low voice. "I was only here as a courtesy."

"What did you think, Elizabeth?" Ben stood and walked around the edge of the desk until he was next to her, staring down at her as if he could see clear through to her soul. "Were you worried about my behavior?"

He was robbing the room of the air around her. She took a deep breath. "Yes."

"Always honest," he said, but it didn't sound like a compliment.

Her old stubbornness came forward. She tilted her chin as if she were a windmill. "I try to be."

As he studied her face, a smile played about his lips, but it didn't reach his eyes. His gaze dropped to her legs before he looked back up at her. "Let's go have a drink."

"No, thank you. I can't."

"A soda then."

She shook her head.

"Why? Haven't you forgiven me for our last argument?"

"I have. But the answer is still no, thank you."

"What about dinner?"

Her heart contracted. She wanted nothing more than to be with Ben, but she knew it wouldn't change his mind about loving her. She didn't need to have her face rubbed in that fact. She couldn't go through another two months like the last. Her reserves of emotional and physical strength were shot. "No, thank you."

Ben rested on the edge of her desk, his long legs stretched out to the side of her. He was so close she could smell his aftershave. She vividly remembered the feel of his arms securely around her, the musky scent of his skin, the tempting taste of his mouth....

"Please." His low voice rumbled through her, filling her with need. "Accept my apology for getting us both into this mess. I wanted you so badly, I was willing to make mistakes. Doesn't that tell you something?"

Her throat closed. She didn't trust her voice so she shook her head.

"Do you hate me that much?"

She couldn't, wouldn't lie. "I love you. But I'm not willing to be your whipping boy every time you decide to lash out. You walk on the edge of constant anger. It's not good for you or me, or for our baby."

Her declaration of love fell on deaf ears. His answering smile more resembled a sneer. "You have a funny way of showing love," he said, folding his arms across his chest.

Defensive again.

"And you don't show love at all." She shrugged, refusing to let him know how much rehashing all this hurt. "So the answer is still no."

Derision was in his tone. "Isn't it a little backward? We've already made love and created a baby. Isn't that enough? Do I have to declare undying love, too?"

"Not unless you mean it."

"Sounds manipulative to me."

She lifted her chin in defiance. "That's your opinion. And don't throw too many judgmental words around."

The silence that followed was electric. Suddenly, Ben lost his starchy anger. He relaxed his shoulders. "I apologize, Elizabeth. I stepped out of bounds."

She wouldn't answer. She couldn't. Every cell in her body hurt from the scorch of his resentment.

Ben stood. "I guess I'd better go before I do any more damage. Will you walk me to the door?"

She began answering him the way she had once before, by telling him he knew where the door was. But she changed her mind. She would see any other client out, so why not him?

But when she stood up, Ben was next to her. His arms snaked around her waist and pulled her against the hardness of his body. "That's more like it." His voice was laced with satisfaction, as if he'd needed to touch her as much as she'd wanted him to hold her.

His body made her feel good, but that didn't make everything all right. She wanted to eat chocolate all the time, but that wasn't good for her, either. Of the two, Ben was by far the most hazardous to her health. He was addictive, labeled Heartbreak.

With all her might, Elizabeth tried to keep her equilibrium. "This isn't necessary, Ben," she said, placing her hands on his chest to keep distance between them. "You don't owe either one of us a second chance. I've accepted that decision."

"Can't I change my mind?"

"Not if you're just testing to see what we're

like together now. Check your memory. It's not right to do this to me on a whim.''

''No, but it sure feels good,'' he replied, his voice going all rough and soft, just the way she remembered it.

Her throat tightened again and tears threatened. Hormones. ''Let me go. Please.''

''In a minute,'' he whispered. ''In a minute.'' He brought his mouth down on hers and bit gently on her bottom lip. Her response was instantaneous and undeniable. The kiss that followed made her fingers curl and she clung to his broad shoulders so she wouldn't fall flat on her face.

She felt his muscled chest through his suit and felt pliable, soft, against his hard body. As his kiss deepened, he pulled her body between his legs and she knew he wanted her as much as she wanted him.

But that wasn't news, and the damage was already done. His seed had already been planted in fertile ground. She didn't need to compound the problem. Yet a small voice inside her head prodded her. *Where is the harm, then? Why not enjoy this small moment?* It could be all she would have to take her through the rest of her life.

Giving in to that thought, she let her arms creep around his neck so she could feel, one last time, his thick hair under her fingers. When his seeking tongue demanded she respond, she did. Joyfully. One last time, without saying the words aloud, Elizabeth told Ben she loved him with all her heart.

His arms tightened, strengthening their bond,

as he pulled her even closer. She felt every soft curve of her body blending with his, every muscle relaxing and molding against him.

It was as much reluctance as it was the need to feel in control that finally pulled her away, which was a war she'd been fighting ever since she'd met Ben Damati.

"Wow," he said, his breathing as harsh as hers. "I thought I knew how good we are together. I was wrong. Reality is much better than memory."

Elizabeth sighed. "This is just an illusion, Ben. In another half hour we'll be fighting again and you'll be withdrawing or angry—either one...."

"Listen," he interjected. "I—"

"No. You listen," she retorted, her own frustration flaring as she realized she was being used, for whatever reason. She had a lot to protect—almost as much as she had love to give. "Acting like an ass is something you can do very well without my interfering. Take charge of your own actions, Ben Damati, before you demand responsibility from others!"

Elizabeth stepped back from him. She needed to put the desk between them or she'd haul off and slug him just for being so damn dense! "I believe this counseling session is over, Mr. Damati. I'll send the bill through the mail."

Ben placed his hands on his hips and glared at her. "Send it to *his* parents. I'm paying Marina to be my counselor, not you."

It was a slap in the face that made her reel from the impact. "I see." She took a deep breath and reached for some semblance of control, her anger palpable in the room, thickening between them like an evening fog. "Goodbye, and thank you for coming today."

Two pairs of eyes locked. Both were vulnerable, both angry. After a silent, tension-filled moment, Ben turned and left the office. He didn't even bother to close the door behind him. She knew then that they'd both gone too far and neither could find their way back.

Elizabeth sank down in her chair and closed her eyes. Exhausted, barely able to move, she rested her head on her crossed arms on the desk. She'd cried so many tears in the past four months, she couldn't conjure up even one more.

Elizabeth Jean Gallagher, who had worked all her life to counsel and warn young women about unplanned pregnancy, was pregnant and unwed.

She had momentarily acted like a confused teenager instead of the grown, professional woman she was, and she felt like a total hypocrite.

All the lessons she'd spouted so often, all that stuff about love needing to be tempered with judgement, had fallen on her own deaf ears.

How ironic.

8

BEN SLAMMED THE PHONE down after bidding farewell to a disgruntled client. He breathed deeply and tried to exhale his anger. Lately, it seemed, he'd been making a habit of flaring up.

Lately? Even if it was only to himself, he had to admit he'd lost his temper a *lot* in the past six years. Everything in his life had become one big irritant. What the hell was the matter with him?

Willing away the ever-present tension seizing his body, Ben pinched the bridge of his nose and closed his eyes. He'd felt this way ever since Elizabeth had walked out of his life. Correction. Ever since he'd *driven* Elizabeth out of his life. He'd done it. He'd blown it. He knew it.

He knew it because his gut told him so.

With Elizabeth, he'd realized how vulnerable he was. He was a big and powerful man until he came home. Then he realized just how extensive his ignorance was and how little he was prepared for. He'd been lucky enough to skim through personal relationships and make it big in his career. Until Elizabeth had pointed it out, he hadn't understood just how easy he'd had it, how much he'd been avoiding as a parent. He'd never delved beyond what he could see, never paid the emotional dues for the love and the life he had.

Elizabeth hadn't and wouldn't let him get by without feeling deeply, feeling everything. All the tension, worry, indecision and heartache would be up front as long as he was with her. So would the heart-stopping, blood-pounding, overwhelming ecstasy he felt with her.

Dealing with Elizabeth and his own, new-found emotions, he'd felt like a rubber ball, bouncing from high to low.

He couldn't blame anyone else for his unhappiness. When it came to Elizabeth, he'd been stupid as dirt. He'd broken off their relationship because he was afraid she—or any other woman—might demand something from him that his money couldn't buy.

He'd never felt so out of control, so he'd run instead of facing things like a man. He'd run away like some damn teenager.

Just like young Steve Bennington.

But he needed Elizabeth back in his life. Hell, he'd been walking around as if he'd lost something precious. And he had. It took time to realize that he was in mourning whenever Elizabeth was out of his arms.

It had all come to a head when he'd returned from meeting with Elizabeth and the father of his grandchild. It was tough enough feeling as hot and stupid as a young stud while looking grand-parenthood in the face. Having to confront the young punk who had taken his place in his daughter's heart made it ten times worse.

Ben went into the kitchen and poured himself

a steep scotch. He wanted it as much to calm his needy reaction to Elizabeth as to fortify himself in the aftermath of his talk with the young man.

It was damn hard facing the truth about himself, which surprised him. He'd always been up front and honest in his business life, able to take any cards that were dealt to him in his personal life. But he was a fraud. He'd acted like a spoiled child who had been found lacking, then taken all his marbles out of the game and refused to play anymore.

He decided it was time to sit down and take a good look at himself. All he had to do was learn whatever it was he needed to know, and then get on with his life. Maybe then he'd be able to smile again. He liked the sound of that. It sounded sane and sensible, especially the getting-on part.

And he knew what the getting-on part was. Damn it!

His fist hit the desk. He wanted things with Elizabeth back the way they were! He'd made a mistake, a stupid mistake when he'd pulled away. He'd been scared and had run. That was all. But he wanted her back now. *Now*. What would it take?

He told himself he was good at coming up with solutions to problems. That was how he'd made a success of his career. Certainly, he should be able to solve this simple, personal dilemma.

He wanted Elizabeth in his life. In his home. In his family. In his arms and his bed. She was already part of him, fueling the fire in his belly that always flared at the mere thought of her.

It was all so simple. He'd finally found love. This was it.

Ben Damati loved Elizabeth Jean Gallagher.

He'd goofed, but that didn't mean the fight was over and he'd lost her forever. He'd learn his lesson and would get her back.

ELIZABETH'S CLOTHING was tight—hard to believe, but true. Her body had found a way to hold on to fat. Finally. She'd always been too thin; she'd always known it, but hadn't expected to keep the weight on this way. Looking in the mirror, she realized she liked the slightly rounded look of her pregnant body; it softened her, made her look more…feminine.

If only Ben could see her now…

The thought of him undressing her, his dark eyes dancing intimately over her skin, filling with awe and wonder… The thought of him touching her, feeling the baby they created and loving the movements…

Once again, Elizabeth shed tears that were ever-present. Tears she told herself were due to the pregnancy.

But that wasn't true.

She missed Ben in her life so much it was a physical hurt. Someday, she told herself, the hurt would fade to an ache, and an ache was something she could deal with.

The telephone buzzed and she flipped the switch. "Yes, Darlene?"

"Mr. Damati is here and wants to know if he can speak to you." Darlene's usually brisk voice held a ton of doubt and hesitancy. "I told him you have another appointment in five minutes, but he insists...."

Elizabeth's heart beat rapidly in her breast. Trying to sound composed, she replied, "Send him in, Darlene."

Nerves jangling, she waited.

She wished she'd put on lipstick, brushed her hair, gone to the bathroom.

She hoped she looked presentable. She hoped he would be kind and not flare up and upset them both. She hoped...

Then, suddenly, he was standing in her office doorway, gazing at her with midnight-dark eyes.

Her throat turned dry.

"Hello, Elizabeth," he said, his voice soft, sexy, private.

She didn't get up from her desk. Instead she reached for the little jar of hopes, as if it were a talisman, and placed it on top of a pile of files. Her hand still resting on the jar, she swallowed and said, "Hello, Ben. How are you?"

He waited what seemed like an hour before answering. "Repentant and asking for your indulgence," he said softly and stepped into the room. He closed the door behind him, but he remained standing there. "If you're going to throw something, please let me know now."

Realizing she was stroking the small jar, she quickly took her hand away. "And then what? You'll leave?"

"No, I'll duck." He stepped toward the empty chair, but didn't sit down. "I'm not leaving until you give me a chance to say my piece. I owe both of us that much."

"You don't owe me anything, Ben," she said, her gaze touching him, seeking to memorize all the planes and angles of his face. She was hungry for him, even though she knew he wasn't good for her. "Please don't feel obligated."

"I feel..." He finally came around the chair and sat down. He shook his head, a rueful smile tilting his lips. He looked so sad she wanted to hold him and tell him that whatever it was it would get better. But she didn't. She couldn't.

"Actually, I'm not sure anymore what I feel, Elizabeth. I've been so blind for so long. So wrong. I need to work those things out."

"What kinds of things?" she asked, afraid to hear the answer.

"I still need to work out my relationship with Barbie. There's so much I want to teach her. Share with her." He leaned closer in the chair. "The only thing she's learned from me is that work comes first and that you can be angry for your entire life. I don't want that for her."

"Barbie's old enough to have her own beliefs, Ben."

"Whatever. I don't think she's equipped to handle life, yet." He leaned back in the chair, his eyes sad and solemn. "But that's not why I'm here. I need to learn to be close to you, Elizabeth. I need to feel your softness. Your love. I need you." He pulled his hands out of his pockets and braced them on her desk. "I need you so much, I'm shaking."

All Elizabeth's hopes were there in that declaration. But it was too late. She needed his love...all of it. He was still just offering a business agreement. This was simply another way for him to get her to marry him.

Her gaze never wavered from his. "Why? So you can put me in a safe place, feel better about yourself and then go off and do your own thing with a clear conscience? So I won't be the only hanging thread in your neat and tidy life?" She shook her head. "No, thanks."

"This is my child, too."

Elizabeth took a deep breath. "You did what you thought was right, Ben. You proposed...I think. I thank you for the honor, but I don't have to accept." Her gaze was distant. "And I don't."

"Why?"

"Because you don't need to be married to play daddy. You'll act responsibly anyway."

"Blunt and honest, that's you," he stated with the saddest smile she'd ever seen. "But I *want* to marry you, damn it! Most women would jump at the chance!"

She raised her brows. "How nice for me."

His smile was sweet and sexy as he came around the desk and took her by the waist, pulling her to her feet. "Come on," he said softly, as if he were baiting a hook. "We can be a happy family."

She loved how it felt to be held by him. These past two months had been tough. She forced herself to remember just *how* tough and what it would be like married to a man who didn't love her.

"Does that mean you're going to grow up?"

"Already did that," he said, withdrawing once more. He stood back, jamming his hands in his pants pockets. "The hard way, in the past two months."

Elizabeth took a deep breath. "Is there an easy way, Ben?"

"You're the counselor. You tell me."

"I can't. I'm *not* you. I've got my own problems."

His forehead furrowed. "I'm taking the blame for my actions, Elizabeth. I lied about the health of my marriage so long, I forgot the truth. I had to face it at last."

"And now what?"

"And now, maybe I can find peace. And we can be together, raising our child."

"Ben—" She couldn't cope with this conversation anymore.

"Hear me out," he urged fervently. "I'm asking you to give me a chance to have you in my life, Elizabeth. Please." He leaned against her desk, his hands splayed on the ink blotter. "I don't want to make the same mistake twice. I don't want to see that cold, distant look in your eyes that I caused in Jeanne's. That same lack of respect. I want us to give to each other freely and without blame. No matter what." He stared down at her, his heated gaze warming her through and through, seeing straight down to the bottom of her soul. "Do you understand what I'm trying to say?"

She nodded, her eyes filled with tears. How many years he must have suffered in his marriage! His speech confirmed just how awful it must have been for him and his wife to be in a marriage that hadn't been built on love. She was thankful not to be in one. She was lucky she didn't have to marry, because living with Ben while he withheld his love would be even more horrible than living without him. "I understand."

"I need to find me again, and I want to do it with you." He gripped the desktop. "Will you give me a chance, Elizabeth?" His gaze pleaded with her. "Please."

She ached with hurt and lost dreams. Why couldn't he have said this before he knew she was pregnant? Why couldn't he have said he loved her? Not once had he done so. Love—that was the one thing she needed from him more than anything else.

Especially now. If he married her without love, he would grow to resent her, and himself, for ending up in the same position twice. If ever he spouted words of love, she wouldn't know whether he loved her for herself or he was just doing the right thing for their child.

She couldn't put herself in that place. No. She didn't trust this new man who said he wanted her in his life. He wasn't the solution.

Her throat closed up with unshed tears, but she remained strong. Not now. This wasn't the time. "I'm sorry."

He closed his eyes for a moment. When he opened them again, his own pain was obvious. "You don't mean that."

Elizabeth looked down at her small jar. His gift of hope. That hope was gone forever. Realizing she had to face him, convince him otherwise until he went away, she stared at him as solemnly as he was staring at her. "I mean it. Please leave."

"I believed what you said. I believed you loved me." He stood straight and tall, as if fending off the arrows of deceit. "I was wrong."

"We both were." She didn't know how much longer she could hold out before breaking down entirely.

He walked to the door and put his hand on the knob, then turned and looked at her, intense hurt in his eyes. "You lied to me, didn't you. You lied about loving me. Why?"

"It doesn't matter now, does it?" she retorted softly. "You don't even know what you want from life, yet you're angry that I won't wait around while you make up your mind."

"I'm being honest."

"Well, so am I," she said, praying her tears wouldn't come yet. She tried to keep the pain at a distance. Not yet...not yet....

He turned the knob, opened the door and walked out. So very controlled.

After the door clicked shut behind him, she sat back in her chair and felt the breath ooze out of her. What had she done?

She'd just turned down the man of her dreams so she could maintain—what? Her self-respect? Her independence? Or, maybe, her own fears?

One tear slipped down her cheek, then another. Within moments, sobs racked her shoulders and haunting sounds tore from her throat. They didn't stop for a long time.

SHE WAS FORCED to cancel her next appointment. She went to the bathroom, washed her face and carefully reapplied her makeup. Then she stared at the woman in the mirror as if she was looking at a stranger, because that was the only way she could keep the lid on her emotions.

She decided it was time to commit herself to continuing with life's little duties. It was time to eat something to keep up her strength. Time to do the laundry. Clean the house. Get enough sleep for tomorrow. She would do one thing after another until she became numb to time itself.

Yet a series of lonely tomorrows stretched ahead. *Not now, not yet*, she said to herself. This wasn't the time to figure out the rest of her life.

Making a quick decision, she called Darlene at the front desk and told her to cancel the rest of her appointments. She picked up her briefcase and purse and walked out the door to her car.

"Count your blessings, Elizabeth Jean," she muttered. At least she had stopped crying. Instead of feeling relieved, she felt empty. Empty except for the tiny new child forming and growing inside her. It gave her something to look forward to. She would have someone to love.

She hoped she would be a good parent, a good teacher, helping her child to get through the world with the least amount of hurt. No matter what, she'd give her child all the love she had.

That night, just before closing her eyes, she decided it was time to take the next step in her life, time to take charge. She had to leave Atlanta and find a place to start again.

BEN STOOD ON THE VERANDA overlooking the back gardens and finished closing the deal of a lifetime. The cell phone glued to his ear, he set up a time for the contract appointment. When he clicked off, he should have felt the rush of satisfaction that came with a good deal signed and sealed, but he didn't. He was numb.

He'd been working on landing this contract for over two years. It had finally happened, and it didn't really matter. Doing business had been no more than a way to focus on something other than his encounter with Elizabeth—an excuse not to relive their conversation.

Now that business was done, he felt his stomach was tied in knots. He was raging mad.

He had humbled himself to the woman of his dreams. What did she do? She turned him down. *Turned him down!*

She acted as if his speech was nothing, as if his words were dry-as-dust rhetoric. She hadn't given a damn what his reasons for hesitation were. She'd simply said no, as if he'd offered her ice cream or peppermints or any other damn triviality.

But it was *his love!*

Anger spilled into his every action as he paced the kitchen. Elizabeth didn't love him. She might have embraced his daughter, but she had lied to him about her love. He reached into the fridge and grabbed an apple.

He was too damn angry to eat crow....

He was angry with himself, too. Ben Damati was in love with Elizabeth Jean Gallagher.

And she didn't give a damn.

As his fist hit the counter in frustration, every

ounce of energy he had was alive, awake and pulsating through his body.

"Daddy?"

Ben jumped. He didn't know how long he'd been standing there, but it must have been awhile. He glanced at his watch. It was just after two a.m. Concern for Barbie shot through him. "What's the matter, honey?"

She stood in the doorway of the kitchen, her fluffy pink bunny slippers matching her pink shortie gown and long white robe. Her hands were on her tummy, and there was a worried frown on her youthful face. "I don't know if anything's wrong, but I'm hurting."

Ben was at her side immediately. "Are you having contractions, honey?" He prayed not. He was prepared to drive to the hospital. Fast. If that was a solution to this problem, he had the answer. If it wasn't...

"No, the baby just punches and makes aches," she said wryly. Her hands soothed her belly as if she could wipe away the pain.

A quick memory flashed through his mind of Jeanne doing the same thing. He blinked several times, that big, lonely ache at being the only one to experience the miracle of the birth of a grandchild turned into a growing pain that centered in his heart. "Come sit down, honey, and I'll make you some warm milk. I used to make it for your mom when she was carrying you and you decided to use her as a punching bag."

Barbie's eyes widened in delight. "Really? Tell me about it," she said as she shuffled over to the table and took a seat.

As Ben prepared hot chocolate, he started talking. It seemed like the most natural thing in the world to spill out all the memories he'd kept bottled up for so many years.

For the first time ever, Ben told his daughter things he'd never shared with her before. He related details about the nights her mom had tossed and turned, how they'd decided to name Barbie, what their arguments were like. He remembered small incidents that he didn't even know he recalled.

Barbie giggled and Ben chuckled with her. She teared up and he actually sat and cried with her. They laughed, and hugged and laughed again. Barbie sometimes wiped his tears as well as her own.

Ben couldn't stop talking. It was as if all those memories had been locked away for all those years and needed to come out at just this time, be a comfort to Barbie when she most needed it.

It was amazing. Walls that had been standing for years finally crumbled.

His daughter had memories of her own to share—some details and incidents. It was odd to think that a moment so important to Barbie-the-child wasn't even a memory in his bank.

Suddenly, Barbie's eyes widened. She carefully placed her cup back in the saucer. "Daddy?" she said, looking like a little girl again.

Then she stood.

Ben thought she had remembered something else and waited expectantly. "Yes, baby?" he prompted.

Her eyes got even bigger, if that were possible.

"Daddy?" Her voice shook with both fear and excitement as she glanced at the kitchen clock. "I think it's time."

No. It couldn't be. He wasn't ready. Not physically. Not emotionally. Not ever. Panic built. He took a deep breath and reached over to pat her hand reassuringly. "Are you sure, Barbie? It could be those, uh, those fake contractions." He hoped. He prayed. Not yet. He wasn't ready yet.

Barbie's breath came out in a whoosh and she gave a laugh. "Nope, Daddy. It's not a Braxton-Hicks. I'm certain. This is the big 'it.' I'll call the doctor and get dressed. Will you get my suitcase? It's in the hall closet."

Ben stared at his little girl, his heart beating so rapidly, he could hardly hear her words over the din.

He was just learning how to be a dad and now he was going to be a grandfather.

He'd never been so scared.

9

ELIZABETH STARED at her bedroom ceiling fan as it lazily circled. For the first time since her pregnancy began, she couldn't fall asleep. She needed to. Hoped to. She was exhausted, but she couldn't shut down. Her mind whirled.

Tears trickled down her cheeks and dampened her pillow. She wanted to blame hormones, but she knew better. She could kid everyone else, but she couldn't kid herself.

She was leaving Atlanta this afternoon, taking the first step to change her life. The decision was made and she was moving to Austin. Starting tomorrow, she would search for an apartment and a clinic she could associate herself with temporarily, until she could establish her own. She had letters of recommendation from the school districts and several of the other authorities and committees she worked through. It wouldn't be hard.

The hard part was that she would be missing Ben Damati for the rest of her life.

The phone rang, shaking her from her sad reverie. She reached for it immediately. It was Ben.

"I'm a grandfather, Elizabeth! Can you believe it?" He sounded thrilled, scared and disbelieving all at the same time. "Barbie delivered at five-thirty this morning."

She curled on her side and held the phone close to her ear. "That's wonderful! Boy or girl?"

"A beautiful eight-pound girl," he stated proudly. "And Barbie's naming her Jeanne Elizabeth, after her mother—and you."

Tears rushed to Elizabeth's eyes. "I'm honored," she whispered, trying to keep from crying. "I'll call her. But when you see her, give her a hug for me?"

"Give her one, yourself. I'll come by and take you over this afternoon."

"No, I…" She had to think fast. Her plane took off just after lunch and she didn't want to have a confrontation with Ben. Not now, anyway. "Can we do it this morning? I have a client to meet this afternoon."

"Cancel the appointment," he said. "This is more important." Silence filled the air. "It is, isn't it?"

"I…I really need to keep this appointment," she lied. "It's very important that I see the woman. She's at the same pivotal point that Barbie was four months ago." Elizabeth didn't mention that the woman was herself. "What hospital is Barbie in?"

"I'll take you," Ben repeated, but his enthusiasm had dwindled. "What time?"

"Ten o'clock," she stated, tightly clutching the phone.

"See you then," he said. "How are you feeling?" His voice softened and his tenderness was her undoing.

A sob caught in her throat and she covered the receiver with her hand so he wouldn't hear.

"Elizabeth? Are you there?"

She took a deep breath and forced herself to relax. Time with Ben was precious. Soon she wouldn't be able to pick up the phone and hear his voice, all soft and sexy. After she moved, she doubted he would be so friendly with her. She tried to put a smile in her voice. "Yes, Ben. I'm here. I'm crying because I'm so touched." She gave a shaky laugh. "You know how women are. We get so emotional."

"I never thought I'd hear you say there's a difference between men and women," he said, obviously surprised. "I thought you demanded equality."

That stopped the tears for a moment. She'd succeeded in diverting even herself from their problems. "I *am* equal. I'm just not the same."

His low, sexy laugh echoed in her ear and stirred her deeply, sexually. "I miss talking to you, Elizabeth," he said, sounding as if he was relating a delicious secret. "You always make me think and never cut me any slack."

"That makes me sound like your teacher."

"Funny," he said slowly. "I thought it sounded like a woman who stands up for herself and what she believes. A woman who has a strong sense of self. The mother of my unborn child."

He didn't add that she was the love of his life. If ever there was a chance to do so, it would have been now. He didn't. It was reinforcement for the move she was making.

"Listen," she said, "someone's at the door. Probably my neighbor. I'll see you later, okay?" Before he could answer, she hung up the phone.

Then the tears began in earnest, but by ten o'clock, she had packed a small bag and placed it in the trunk of her car. The house was ready to lock up for the three days she'd be gone. The realtor was setting up the For Sale sign on her lawn tomorrow and was optimistic about an early sale. Before leaving, Elizabeth wrote a hope and placed it in the jar that was on top of the coffee table. She'd brought it home from work along with most of her personal effects.

She was waiting outside when Ben drove up. With a bright smile, she stepped to the car. "I'll follow you," she said when he opened his door. He looked at her with several questions in his dark eyes.

"Why?" he said, getting out and giving her a hug in greeting. It was unlike him to give friendly hugs, but she didn't mind at all.

She hugged him back, feeling his strength. She was as reluctant to let him go as she thought she'd be. Instead, she allowed her hands to drift to his shoulders and smooth the fabric of his casual sports shirt. She needed the feel of him in her arms...if only for a little while. She forced herself back to reality. "I have an appointment, remember? The sooner we get going, the longer I can enjoy my visit."

"Can't I drop you off at your appointment and pick you up later?" He rubbed the small of her back and the tops of her hips, his warm hands easing her tight muscles and making her heart race at the same time. "That way we can talk for a little while." He grinned engagingly. "And maybe I can persuade you to have dinner with me."

She cleared her throat. "I can't. I need my car. I'm having dinner with a friend."

He stiffened just enough for her to notice, his expression guarded. "Male?"

"None of your business."

"It is if he's planning on being in your life," he stated with finality. "You're carrying my child."

Elizabeth pulled back. "I know that even better than you do, Ben, but that doesn't give you any right to tell me who to eat with." Her voice sounded bitter and she softened it. "You really don't have a right to ask."

"I think I do. Besides, I've asked you to marry me so many times I'm embarrassed to mention it anymore. If you turned me down for some snot-nosed—"

"Don't even go there," Elizabeth interrupted in a warning voice.

He glared in answer.

She took a deep breath. He looked as angry as she felt. It seemed that everything escalated out of control when they were together. They both wanted commitment, but she needed it along with his love. That wasn't going to happen.

But they couldn't part this way. If she had lied this much, she might as well continue. "Don't worry. It's a girlfriend."

The stiffness went out of him. "Sorry. You're right. I don't have a right to know. Not yet."

As she began to disagree, his mouth covered

hers in a light kiss. "But I will. Eventually, I'll wear you down like water on rock. And you won't be sorry when we marry. I promise."

"I'm not surprised, since you won't be my husband," she stated as casually as she could manage. She hoped it sounded as if she was making a joke. Without checking his reaction, she walked to her own car as she palmed her keys. "Let's get going."

BARBIE WAS MORE THAN ready to show off her new charge. She bubbled over with excitement and was filled with a confidence that was astounding.

"I'm taking care of Jeanne Elizabeth every hour. She sleeps at the foot of my bed and I can hear her twist and turn. She makes the most wonderful little noises," she enthused. "And the nurses have almost as many answers as that class you made me take on child care, Elizabeth."

"She's beautiful," Elizabeth said. "And I'm honored you named her after me."

Elizabeth's hand stayed clasped in Barbie's for most of the visit, except when Elizabeth held the baby. The infant clutched Elizabeth's finger with a strength that was both astonishing and sweet. Those same tiny fingers invisibly wrapped around her heart.

After they left the hospital, Elizabeth and Ben went their separate ways. She had to keep telling herself why she was doing this instead of running into his arms and demanding he take care of her and their child.

She loved Ben and had enough pride in herself

to walk away. He didn't need to be "caught" in a loveless marriage twice, and Elizabeth needed love more than she needed air to breathe or water to drink.

She wished Ben was a complete heel. It would be so much easier to leave him if he wasn't so lovable.

Elizabeth placed a hand over her rounded belly. That was all right. This baby was *hers.* It didn't matter that she wasn't married or that she had made the biggest professional mistake in her life by doing exactly what she preached against.

It didn't matter that she would have to work twice as hard to support two instead of one.

This baby was hers!

She felt so protective of the new life growing bigger and stronger every day. "I love you so much," she silently told her baby. "And I'll find a way to make up for not having your daddy around all the time."

It was for the best.

The sadness caught up with her once more, making her cry all the way to the airport, but she didn't turn the car around.

THE NEXT MORNING, Ben woke up ready to storm over to Elizabeth Jean's house and force her to take him and his proposal seriously. But by mid-morning, he'd changed his mind, worried she would cut him off completely if she felt threatened. By midafternoon he was angry with himself for backing off, and wanted to yell, hit a wall, scream to the gods.

He did none of those things—but he wanted to.

Two days after giving birth, Barbie was home from the hospital and consumed with the baby. Her friends poured into the house in a constant stream. The nanny Ben had hired was young enough to deal with the teenage traffic and experienced enough to care for the baby as well. Barbie tended Jeanne Elizabeth as if she'd been doing it all her young life.

Ben fell in love with his grandbaby the first time he held her, and there was no going back. Whenever he had the chance, he rocked her, talked to her and told her what the world had in store for such a beautiful child as she.

And then he wondered what his own child—his child with Elizabeth—would look like. But he already knew; a child of Elizabeth's would glow with an overflow of devotion. But the child was both of theirs. He'd do things differently this time. Never again would he live on the outskirts of his child's life as he had with Barbie; he'd be an integral part of this child's everyday life from the moment it was born.

Suddenly he realized that was what he wanted more than anything in the world, and he was willing to fight for it with everything he had. He was smart enough to learn. He was smart enough to love—and to express that love every day.

He was smart enough to show Elizabeth Jean Gallagher that he deserved to be in her life.

When he called Elizabeth the next day, he got

the answering machine. For three days, he left messages.

With each passing day, he made more plans....

Ben's mother and Flynn visited to meet the new baby. Linda didn't want the responsibility of regularly taking care of little Jeanne, but she wanted to be a part of her life, which suited everyone just fine.

Flynn hemmed and hawed before finally sticking his head in the study door where Ben was sketching a few new concepts for a prison pod he was designing for a conglomerate in Nice, France. "Have you got a minute, son?"

"Sure. Come on in," Ben said, welcoming the diversion. He placed his pencils on the drafting table. "I've got soft drinks. Want one?"

Flynn gave him a wry look. "No, thanks."

"Beer?"

"Now you're talkin'."

Ben reached behind his desk, where a small built-in fridge held the soft drinks and a couple of beers.

He popped the top on a can and handed it to Flynn, then got one for himself. Once they were seated in the overstuffed morris chairs flanking the fireplace, he took a long drink. "What's on your mind?" he finally prompted.

"You are, my boy." Flynn stared at him. Hard. "I used to think you had all the answers. Knew what to do and when to do it."

"Thanks," Ben said. "Obviously I've slipped up somewhere or we wouldn't be having this conversation." He thought back to the last couple of times he'd talked to his mother, but couldn't remember anything unusual there. "What did I do to disillusion you?"

"The way you're handling this 'Lizabeth thing."

Ben's hand tightened on the beer can. "What thing?"

"That's just it. You haven't made a move to get her into this house. You know. Like marriage?"

Ben wasn't surprised. Flynn was always outspoken. "She doesn't want to get into this house. She's turned me down. So far."

Flynn gave a hefty sigh. "You know, your mother turned me down several times. But I didn't take no for an answer, thank God. I kept trying until I won."

Ben remembered. In the beginning, his mother had tried to stay out of Flynn's way. He was too persistent and overbearing, she had said.

"If I hadn't kept pushing, we'd both be single—and lonely—right now."

"I know, but—"

"And then, when it came to marriage, I refused to let her back away. She had no choice but to marry me."

"But…"

The older man wasn't listening. He was on a roll. "And that's what you need to do with 'Lizabeth, boy. You're giving her too many choices. She doesn't need to run the show, you know. You have a big say-so in this. Maybe you'd better start acting like it."

Ben took another drink. "So far, she won't listen." He sounded like a whiner. Hell, right now he *was* a whiner!

Flynn leaned forward. "*Make* her listen, boy! A woman *likes* a man who takes command of a situation. Instead, she's gettin' away and you're bein' nice about it!"

Ben silently agreed, but wasn't sure what avenues were open to him. He knew better than to act like a caveman and lose her. "I'm just giving her time to sort things through. That's all."

"Then what's the For Sale sign doing in her front yard?" Flynn stared at him, gauging his reactions.

Ben went cold. His heart stopped beating, then began an irregular thumping. "What?"

"There's a For Sale sign in her yard," Flynn explained patiently. "We went by on our way here this morning. Linda wanted to say hi before coming over. Seems that 'Lizabeth called to congratulate her the day little Jeanne was born," Flynn said.

"Are you sure?"

"I'm sure." Flynn nodded in confirmation. "She's moving away from here, Ben."

The beer can collapsed in Ben's crushing grip. He looked at his own hand as if it belonged to someone else. "Thanks, Flynn." He stood. "Excuse me. I think I'll take a drive."

"Have at it, my boy. Take no prisoners." But Flynn was talking to Ben's back.

TEN MINUTES LATER, Ben was glaring at the realtor's sign and stomping up the walk. He rang the doorbell, pounded on the door, but there was no answer. He walked around the back and peered through the kitchen window. The room was spotless. As if nobody lived there. Obviously, she'd been gone awhile.

Unfolding his small cellular phone, Ben dialed her number. The answering machine came on. With hands that shook in anger, he listened to the message, then gave one back in the sexiest, most innocent voice he could summon.

"Hi, Elizabeth, darlin'. It's Ben. I can't wait to see you again. I'm counting the days." And for the first time, he said the words he hadn't said before. "I love you." It was the commitment of his lifetime.

He dialed the realtor's number next and asked to see the house. The agent promised to meet him there in fifteen minutes. It was the longest fifteen minutes of his life. When she got there, they went through the house room by room. She explained all the features Elizabeth had updated and what she'd added to the small house. Ben hadn't known Elizabeth had done so much of the renovation herself.

But he *did* know she was serious about moving. There were dozens of neatly packed boxes stacked against the walls, ready for transport. The more he saw the angrier he got. Damn the woman! She thought she was leaving! With his child!

She had always talked about being up front and honest, but here she was, ready to sneak out in the middle of the night.

The realtor, a Mrs. Doyle, smiled at Ben occasionally, but his attention was focused on the house. He was completely preoccupied with

Elizabeth and any information Mrs. Doyle had that might shed light on what was happening.

"When will it be ready for occupancy?" he finally asked.

"Well, the owner is moving her furniture to Austin in two days, then the painters will be here for three days," she said thoughtfully. "I'd say within two weeks."

"I see." His tone was so grim the woman looked startled. Ben softened the effect with a smile. "Thanks. I'll think about it."

Mrs. Doyle tried to interest him in other properties, but he'd seen what he needed to see. He had the information he was after.

Before he left, he dropped a little piece of paper in the hopes jar, exchanging it for the one that was in there.

ELIZABETH WAS EXHAUSTED. She'd been gone three full days. She wasn't sure, but she thought she might have seen every apartment in Austin. On the upside, Virginia had called Mary Ellen in Houston and the three sisters had spent the evening together. It had been wonderful for Elizabeth to see them again, but heartbreaking to realize just how happy they were in their marriages and that she never would be. Not without Ben.

She knew better than to dwell on her sadness, though.

Her mind was made up. She was leaving Atlanta and beginning a new life. She would not, under any circumstances, set up either herself or Ben for failure by forcing him into a marriage because of a baby. It hadn't worked for Ben the first time. It certainly wouldn't work any better this time.

When the plane landed in Atlanta at eleven-thirty that night, she was on her last legs. Within minutes of entering the house, she'd listened to her messages, then stripped and went to bed. Moments later she was asleep, dreaming of Ben and his soft voice telling her how much he loved and missed her and looked forward to seeing her, how he was waiting for her to call.

He'd said he loved her. They were the most wonderful three words in the English language...if only she hadn't been pregnant when he'd said them.

Thankfully, that was one confrontation she wouldn't have to endure. She had the movers coming in the morning, and by the time Ben realized she was gone, she would be in her new apartment, halfway across the country.

It was a coward's way out, she'd told herself often enough. But she was doing it for both of them. No, all three of them.

ELIZABETH AWOKE groggy and disoriented. Sun blazed through the curtains and spilled into the room. With a sense of urgency to get the moving done in a hurry, she scuffled into the kitchen and started a pot of coffee, then showered while it was brewing. She wanted to fall asleep in the shower, but was able to stay awake long enough to wash her hair and revive herself. After slipping into a loose cotton warm-up suit, she sank to the couch with a cup of hot brew and watched the news.

She'd get used to Texas, she told herself. Just six years ago, she hadn't known anyone in Georgia, either, except for her partner Marina, whom she'd met in college.

Elizabeth was leaving in a day. She still had some loose ends to tie up. She had to make sure she briefed her partners about the clients she was transferring to them.

The small ceramic jar with Hopes written on it sat in the center of the coffee table. She stared at it, picked it up, hoping...nothing. There was so much to do, and here she was, without energy. Without hope.

She was about to put the jar back when the doorbell rang. She was still clutching it when she opened the door and found Ben staring back at her. Suddenly, she was filled with enough energy to run very far away.

"Come on, Elizabeth. Let me in," Ben said.

Wishing she were anywhere else, she kept a death grip on the door handle.

They stared at each other through the screen, neither saying a word for a long time.

"Aren't you even going to offer me a cup of coffee?" Ben finally said, his voice soft as a caress.

"Of course," Elizabeth murmured, finally moved to action. If she bluffed her way through this meeting, maybe she'd get away scot-free. Her thoughts began racing, her instincts alternating between fight and flight. All the boxes were in the garage and bedrooms, not in the living area. Two were in the kitchen, but she could explain those.

She glanced at her watch. The movers weren't due until nine-thirty. She had an hour and a half.

Ben followed her into the kitchen. With shaking hands, she reached for a cup, but he took it away from her hands and filled it himself. Then, with one hip against the kitchen counter, he tasted the brew. His expression was bland, but his eyes were intimate and loving, and watched her as if she were his bride.

Elizabeth sighed, attempting to calm her breath and her thoughts. She smiled. "What brings you here?"

"Aren't you going to say how much you missed me, darling?"

"I missed you, Ben," she whispered, drinking in the sight of him.

"Hello, and I missed you, too, Elizabeth." His gaze hardened. "I drove by to check on your house and saw your car. I also noticed a For Sale sign in your yard. You're not leaving, are you?"

"I, uh—I'm not sure." She had never stuttered in her life, but she was doing it now.

He dropped his Mr. Nice Guy facade. "You think you're leaving, don't you?" he demanded.

Something in Elizabeth snapped. She wasn't going to be cornered by anyone. Nor intimidated. She was free to move if she wanted to and smart enough to know when it was time to fold her cards. She stood just a little taller. "I *am* leaving, Ben. I'm moving away and beginning again somewhere else."

"Why?"

"That's none of your business."

It seemed she had uttered the very words that would drive Ben over the edge. His expression dark, he took one slow step at a time toward her, stalking her around the kitchen. "It's none of my business who you have dinner with." He took another step. "It's none of my business what you're doing and with whom." He stopped when she was against the kitchen counter and he was directly in front of her. "And now you think it's none of my business where you live."

"We're both adults, Ben—"

She never had a chance to elaborate on whatever her point was. In fact, she forgot her point entirely as Ben's mouth claimed hers in a kiss that made her forget *everything*. With his hands clamped on her hips, he pulled her toward him and showed her just how much he wanted her.

His mouth moved over hers as if he was ravenous for her kisses.

His hands roamed as if he couldn't touch her enough.

His body moved against hers as if he couldn't believe she was in his arms.

And when he gave a low, aching moan, she knew he still wasn't getting enough of her.

And she wasn't getting enough of him, either.

When he pulled away, they were both breathless.

His eyes blazed with messages she couldn't comprehend. She felt confused. Unsure. Overwhelmed.

"Listen to me and listen hard, Elizabeth. I've tried everything else to make you realize just what you're passing up by not marrying me, and it hasn't worked. This tactic has just as much of a chance as anything else. I'm tired of pussy-footing around."

Her eyebrows rose. "Oh, really?"

"Yes, really," he said, steel in his tone. "You're not going anywhere. If you even make a phone call in an attempt to leave, I'll slap a restraining order on you until you come to your senses."

"And when do you think that will be?"

"When you wake up and realize you're passing up the marriage of a lifetime," he snapped. "You're never going to find anyone who loves you more, who will take care of you better, who will try to please you as often. Never. I don't give a damn what you say."

Her eyes widened. "And when was it you decided you love me?" She narrowed her gaze. "I'll tell you when. When you found out I was going to have your child. And, because we come as a package deal, you've decided you can say the words and I'll feel better about stepping into a loveless marriage. Isn't that right?"

"I've loved you since forever." His hands tightened on her hips. "But you didn't want to hear any of that, did you? You didn't want to know why I ran so far and so fast, but I'll tell you now. The love I felt for you—*feel* for you—scared the ever-lovin' hell out of me. But you didn't want to hear that. You've told me at every turn just exactly what you think of men and marriage and commitment, and how women can make it on their own. Well, maybe you're right as far as careers go, but not where love is concerned.

Grown men and women have to admit they love each other and then come to terms with that love. For me, it was the scariest thing in the world. For you, it seemed to be business as usual."

Elizabeth's heart began to beat in that familiar rhythm—the one it took up whenever Ben was around. She told herself that she didn't believe him, that he was selling himself and she certainly didn't have to buy his story. She knew better. He was a very smart man. He knew exactly what words to say to elicit whatever response he wanted.

Just the same. A small part of her wanted to believe so very badly. He was so open, so vulnerable. "Interesting theory. How are you going to prove that?"

"I'm not," he said simply. "I couldn't convince you it was Monday if you had the calendar in your hand. If there's one thing I've learned, it's that you have to be prepared to believe."

"And how will that happen?" she asked, her voice a little softer.

"I don't know yet," he muttered, sounding frustrated. "I haven't figured it out. But I will, Elizabeth. Mark my words, I will."

"You said you love me."

"Hell, that's not news," he growled. "I love you with all my heart and soul. I've never loved like this before in my life and I never will again. And you've already admitted that you love me. What I can't figure out is why in the hell you would turn your back on something that's so wonderful for both of us."

"Because..." She stopped. She was back where

she started. "None of this matters. Nothing will change."

Ben backed her into the counter, his body pressing gently against hers, simply making her aware of him. The tension in his shoulders and neck belied the easy pressure of his body against hers. "You made *me* matter again, when you told me you loved me. Now, talk to me about whatever it is that's making you run." He kissed the top of her head. "And believe that I love you. I want to be with you for the rest of my life. I want you to carry my children and make love to me on bright sunny days and under the stars late at night. I want you to argue with me when you feel you need to and agree with me when you know I'm right. And most of all, I want you to love me with everything you've got, because I need that from you so badly I can't stand the thought of living without it."

His hand came up to stroke her throat, and she swallowed the large lump that was making it impossible to speak. "Why are you running away? What's got you spooked?" His voice was soft. Mesmerizing. Convincing.

But still his past with Jeanne stood between them like the Great Wall of China. Elizabeth couldn't stand to be hurt by him. It was easier to walk away now than to be kicked away later.

"Please," she said, practically begging. "Let me think about it."

Ben smiled. "I'll give you until tomorrow morning. No longer. Meanwhile, don't leave. Do anything like that, and I'll take every action open to me. I *will* take the baby away from you until you come to your senses, Elizabeth. Maybe if I do that, you'll understand that what I really want is you. With me. And I know you'd never leave the baby. Understand. I'm not kidding."

He cupped her head and tilted it slightly. His mouth came down, gently nibbling on her bottom lip before his tongue caressed the soft inside. Her breath disappeared; her heart pumped harder than it ever had before. She wrapped her arms around his waist and held on for dear life. As the kiss deepened, she sighed in surrender, enjoying every nuance of Ben Damati.

He pulled away then, his smile wolfish as he gave her a wink. "I'll see you tomorrow."

After one more light kiss on her mouth, he was gone. Elizabeth Jean Gallagher, usually so together, so confident, so knowing, was no longer any of those things. She collapsed in a kitchen chair and stared down at the checkered linoleum. There was no doubt about it. She felt as if she were standing in front of one door marked Tiger and another marked Loneliness without Ben. Both were dangerous. And she was very confused....

WHEN BEN REACHED the stop sign at the end of Elizabeth's block, he punched in some numbers on the cell phone and waited impatiently for his call to be answered. When it was, he got right to the point. "Marina, this is Ben. I think your friend Elizabeth needs you." He gave her a brief rundown of what had just transpired without telling her he knew about the baby.

Once that conversation was over, he dialed

Judge Raeburn. The judge was an old friend who owed him a favor.

Ben had set the wheels in motion, now, just in case....

ELIZABETH STARED at her little Hopes jar. Ben had given it to her such a long time ago.... She reached for it, and after taking off the flat, fat cork on top, stared down inside.

There was a piece of folded paper sitting on the bottom. Elizabeth frowned. It wasn't the same color as the message she'd put in a few days ago. She upturned the jar and the paper drifted to the table.

She recognized Ben's distinctive handwriting. It was neat, precise, much like the architect he was.

It was dated. He'd obviously left it several days ago.

"I hope Elizabeth loves me half as much as I love her and lets me prove it by marrying me," she read.

Tears welled in her eyes.

She had to be the biggest, stupidest fool in the world if she didn't call him and say yes right away. There was no chance that the man who'd written this note would be a man who could resent her pregnancy. The proof was right here, in this jar.

He loved her enough to step out and take a chance at being rejected. She could do no less.

Hopefully, he'd grown up. Hopefully, so had *she.*

It was time to stop being afraid of loving and losing.

Elizabeth picked up the phone and dialed Ben's cellular number. He answered, his voice crisp and decisive.

"Ben? I love you. And I'll need you to show me just how much you love me every single day until I finally believe it...."

His deep rich laughter was triumphant. "Thank God you came to your senses, woman. I'm too valuable to be dumped."

"And Ben? I want to wait a little while before the ceremony." She hadn't meant to blurt it out. She wanted her sisters to fly in. Her family.

"Sure, but not long." His voice was thick and sexy.

"When?"

"Tomorrow. That'll give you one whole day today to be single. We'll get married by a judge friend of mine. So find two dresses, woman. One for tomorrow and one for tonight. I'll be there to pick you up for dinner at seven."

"Yes, dear," she said, her docile tone hardly hiding her laughter. So much for waiting. Her sisters would just have to drop everything and fly in tomorrow morning.

"Your meek act doesn't fool me, Elizabeth. Every day, you'll probably shoot sparks in every direction. And I'll love every bit of it."

"I love you," she said softly. Then voiced her one concern. "Are you worried about our having a baby?"

"I'm proud of our baby, Elizabeth." His voice was thick with emotion. "I never thought feeling this much love was possible. And to think you're giving me the gift of *another* person to love...."

He paused for a moment and Elizabeth felt tears stinging her eyes. But this time they were tears of happiness.

"When I looked at little Jeanne Elizabeth, I knew that I had to make you understand just how important love is to me," he told her.

"I know. I believe you. And I'm so thankful."

"I'm on my way, darling. Be there."

Her heart leaped in her breast. "Always."

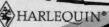

This January Harlequin is proud to present

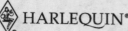

HARLEQUIN®

Escapade

REBECCA YORK
VICKI LEWIS THOMPSON
MARGOT EARLY
LYNNE GRAHAM

This is a special collection of four complete novels for one low price. Featuring four novels from our most popular lines: Harlequin Temptation, Harlequin Intrigue, Harlequin Superromance and Harlequin Presents.

Available at your favorite retail outlet.

HARLEQUIN®

Makes any time special.™

Temptation®

COMING NEXT MONTH

#717 MACKENZIE'S WOMAN JoAnn Ross
Bachelor Auction, Book 1
Alex MacKenzie: Sexy, 6'2", dark-haired adventurer... He was the perfect man for the charity bachelor auction—and Kate Campbell was determined to track him down. So what if they'd once had the shortest marriage in history? Alex was a *very* eligible bachelor and Kate was even tempted to bid on him herself!

#718 CLUB CUPID Stephanie Bond
A tropical holiday was never on workaholic Frankie Jenson's agenda. So what was she doing stranded in Key West wit sexy-as-sin Randy Tate? The gorgeous bar owner tempted her to let loose, indulge in a few island fantasies. Little did Frankie guess that Randy was planning to indulge in a few fantasies of his own....

#719 HER DESPERADO Alyssa Dean
Lacy Johnson's ranch was on the verge of bankruptcy—a marriage of convenience to Morgan Brillings was the *only* solution. Suddenly Lacy found herself looking at her fiancé with new eyes, noticing the sexy cowboy's smiles and wicked way of kissing. But did Morgan see her as anything *more* than a convenient wife?

#720 BLACK VELVET VALENTINES Carrie Alexander Blaze
Our Valentine's gift to you—a collection of three steamy stories:
Secrets of the Heart, in which a caveman becomes a prince to the heroine; **Two Hearts,** featuring seduction by love potion that works all too well...on the wrong man; and **Heart's Desire,** where a fantasy vacation becomes a voyage of sensual discovery.